CHRISTMAS STORIES

CHRISTMAS STORIES

MERCIER PRESS
Cork
www.mercierpress.ie

© The Estate of John B. Keane, 2004

ISBN: 978 1 78117 747 1

10 9 8 7 6 5 4 3 2 1

Some of these stories were originally published in Christmas Tales, The Voice of an Angel, A Christmas Surprise and A Christmas Omnibus.

A CIP record for this title is available from the British Library

Contents

The Curriculum Vitae

Fred Spellacy would always remember the Christmas he spent as a pariah, not for the gloom and isolation it brought him nor for the abuse. He would remember it as a period of unprecedented decision-making which had improved his lot in the long term.

Fred Spellacy believed in Christmas. Man and boy it had fulfilled him and for this he was truly grateful. Of late his Christmases had been less happy but he would persevere with his belief, safe in the knowledge that Christmas would never really let him down.

'Auxiliary Postman Required'. The advertisement, not so prominently displayed on the window of the sub post office, captured Dolly Hallon's attention. Postmen are nice, Dolly thought, and they're kind and, more importantly, everybody respects them. In her mind's eye she saw her father with his postbag slung behind him, his postman's cap tilted rakishly at the side of his head, a smile on his face as he saluted all and sundry on his way down the street.

If ever a postmaster, sub or otherwise, belied his imperious title that man was Fred Spellacy. It could be fairly said that he was the very essence of deferentiality. He was also an abuse-absorber. When things went wrong his superiors made him into a scapegoat, his customers rounded on him, his wife upbraided him, his in-laws chided him. His assistant Miss Finnerty clocked reproachfully as though she were a hen whose egg-laying had been precipitately disrupted. She reserved all her clocking for Fred. She never clocked at Fred's wife but then nobody did.

'Yes child?' Fred Spellacy asked gently.

'It's the postman's job sir.'

Fred Spellacy nodded, noted the pale, ingenuous face, the threadbare clothes.

'What age are you?' he asked gently.

'Eleven,' came the reply, 'but it's not for me. It's for my father.'

'Oh!' said Fred Spellacy.

Dolly Hallon thought she detected a smile. Just in case, she forced one in return.

'What's his name, age and address child?'

'His name is Tom Hallon,' Dolly Hallon replied. 'His age is thirty-seven and his address is Hog Lane.'

Fred Spellacy scribbled the information onto a jotter which hung by a cord from the counter. He knew Tom Hallon well enough. Not a ne'er-do-well by any means, used to work in the mill before it closed. He recalled having heard somewhere that the Hallons were honest. Honest! Some people had no choice but to be honest while others didn't have the opportunity to be dishonest.

'Can he read and write?'

'Oh yes,' Dolly assured him. 'He reads the paper every day when Mister Draper next door is done with it. He can write too! He writes to his sister in America.'

'And Irish? Has he Irish?'

'Oh yes,' came the assured response from the eleven year old. 'He reads my school books. He has nothing else to do!'

'Well Miss Hallon here's what you must get your father to do. Get him to apply for the job and enclose a reference from someone in authority such as the parish priest or one of the teachers. I don't suppose he has a curriculum vitae!'

'What's that?' Dolly Hallon asked, her aspirations unexpectedly imperilled.

'The jobs he's had, his qualifications ...'

Fred Spellacy paused as he endeavoured to find words which might simplify the vacant position's requirements.

'Just get him to put down the things he's good at and don't delay. The position must be filled by noon tomorrow. Christmas is on top of us and the letters are mounting up.'

Dolly Hallon nodded her understanding and hurried homewards.

Fred Spellacy was weary. It was a weariness imposed, not by the demands of his job but by the demands of his wife and by the countless recommendations made to him on behalf of the applicants for the vacant position. Fred Spellacy's was a childless family but there was never a dull moment with Fred's wife Alannah always on the offensive and Fred the opposite.

Earlier that day he had unwittingly made a promise to one of the two local TDs that he would do all within his power for the fellow's nominee. Moments later the phone rang. It was the other TD. Fred had no choice but to make the same promise.

'Don't forget who put you there in the first place!' the latter had reminded him.

Worse was to follow. The reverend mother from the local convent had called, earnestly beseeching him not to forget her nominee, a genuine vessel of immaculacy who was, she assured him, the most devout Catholic in the parish. Hot on her heels came others of influence, shopkeepers, teachers and even a member of the civic guards, all pressed into service by desperate job-seekers who would resort to anything to secure the position. Even the pub next door, which had always been a *sanctum sanctorum*, was out of bounds. The proprietor, none more convivial or more generous, had poured him a double dollop of Power's Gold Label before entreating him to remember one of his regulars, a man of impeccable character, unparalleled integrity, unbelievable scholarship and, to crown all, one of the lads as well!

'Come in here!' There was no mistaking the irritation in his wife's voice. She pointed to a chair in the tiny kitchen.

'Sit down there boy!' She turned her back on him while she lit a cigarette. Contemptuously she exhaled, revelling in the dragonish jets issuing from both nostrils.

Fred sat with bent head, a submissive figure. He dared not even cross his legs. He did not dare to tell her that there were customers waiting, that the queue at the counter was lengthening. He knew that a single word could result in a blistering barrage.

'Melody O'Dea,' she opened, 'is one of my dearest friends.'

Her tone suggested that the meek man who sat facing her would grievously mutilate the woman in question given the slightest opportunity.

Again she drew upon the cigarette. A spasm of coughing followed. She looked at Fred as though he had brought it about.

'Her char's husband Mick hasn't worked for three years.'

Alannah Spellacy proceeded in a tone unused to interference, 'so you'll see to it that he gets the job!'

She rose, cigarette in mouth, and drew her coat about her.

'I'll go down now,' she announced triumphantly, 'and tell Melody the good news!'

When Tom Hallon reported for work at the sub post office at noon the following day Alannah Spellacy was so overcome with shock that she was unable to register a single protest. When Tom Hallon donned the postman's cap, at least a size too large, she disintegrated altogether and had to be helped upstairs, still speechless, by her husband and Miss Finnerty. There she would remain throughout the Christmas, her voice fully restored and to be heard reverberating all over the house until she surprisingly changed her tune shortly after Christmas when it occurred to her that the meek were no longer meek and must needs be cossetted.

Alannah had come to the conclusion that she had pushed her husband as far as he would be pushed. Others would come to the same realisation in due course. Late in his days, but not too late, Fred Spellacy the puppet would be replaced by a resolute, more independent Fred.

Fred had agonised all through the previous night over the appointment. In the beginning he had formed the opinion that it would be in his best interest to appoint the applicant with the most powerful patron but unknown to him the seeds of revolt had been stirring in his subconscious for years. Dolly Hallon had merely been the catalyst.

Fred had grown weary of being told what to do and what not to do. The crisis had been reached shortly after Dolly had walked out the door of the post office.

That night, as he pondered the merits of the score or so applicants, he eventually settled on a shortlist of four. These were the nominees of the two TDs, his wife's nominee and the rank outsider, Tom Hallon, of Hog Lane.

He had once read that the ancient Persians never made a major judgement without a second trial. They judged first when they were drunk and they judged secondly when they were sober. As he left the post office Fred had already made up his mind. He by-passed his local and opted instead for the privacy of a secluded snug in a quiet pub which had seen better days. After his third whiskey and chaser of bottled stout he was assumed into that piquant if temporary state which only immoderate consumption of alcohol can induce.

From his inside pocket he withdrew Tom Hallon's curriculum vitae and read it for the second time. Written on a lined page neatly extracted from a school exercise book it was clearly the work of his daughter Dolly. The spelling was correct but the accomplishments were few. He had worked in the mill but nowhere else. He had lost his job through no fault of his own. Thus far it could have been the story of any unemployed man within a radius of three miles but then the similarities ended for it was revealed that Tom Hallon had successfully played the role of Santa Claus for as long as Dolly could remember. While the gifts he delivered were home-made and lacking in craftsmanship his arrival had brought happiness unbounded to the Hallon family and to the several other poverty-stricken families in Hog Lane.

'Surely,' Fred addressed himself in the privacy of the snug, 'if this man can play the role of Santa Claus then so can I. If he can bear gifts I can bear gifts.'

He rose and buttoned his coat. He pulled up his socks and finished his stout before proceeding unsteadily but resolutely towards the abode of Dolly Hallon in Hog Lane.

He had been prepared, although not fully, for the repercussions. The unsuccessful applicants, their families, friends and handlers, all made their dissatisfaction clear in the run-up to Christmas. They had cast doubts upon his integrity and ancestry in language so malevolent and scurrilous that he was beyond blushing by the time all had had their say.

One man had to be physically restrained and the wife of another had spat into his face. He might not have endured the sustained barrage at all but for one redeeming incident. It wanted but three days for Christmas. A long queue had formed at the post office counter, many of its participants hostile, the remainder impatient.

From upstairs came the woebegone cronawning of his obstructive spouse and when the cronawning ceased there came, down the stairs, shower after shower of the most bitter recriminations, sharper and more piercing than driving hail. He was very nearly at the end of his tether.

'Yes!' he asked of the beaming face which now stood at the head of the ever-lengthening queue. There was no request for stamps nor was there a parcel to be posted. Dolly Hallon just stood there, her pale face transformed by the most angelic and pleasing of smiles. She uttered not a single word but her gratitude beamed from her radiant countenance.

Fred Spellacy felt as though he had been included in the communion of saints. His cares vanished. His heart soared. Then, impassively, she winked at him. Fred Spellacy produced a handkerchief and loudly blew his nose.

A Cock for Christmas

As well as being a Christmas tale the following is also a story of romance, love and no little debauchery from the bird world. As stories go it is as true as any and it happened in my native town some time between the disappearance of the swallowtail coat and the closure of the Lartigue Railway.

It so happened that two young ladies of the so-called Ascendancy classes arrived at the Arms Hotel one September morning and asked if they might see the manager. In carefully cultivated tones from a mixture of non-Celtic origins they informed him that they required the services of the porter. On being assured that he was available they gave instructions that he was to go at once to the local railway station.

There he would collect a crate which had come all the way from Paris. The crate contained two French doves, gentler than a summer dawn and whiter than the untrodden snow.

Duly, the porter returned to the hotel where he deposited the crate upon a reading table in the foyer.

The young misses of the long-since ousted Ascendancy were delighted and, assuming that the birds must surely be starving procured, again with the aid of the porter, the appropriate birdseed.

The doves, however, refused to dine so it was decided that they should be taken from the crate and examined. Great care was taken since it was widely accepted even then that birds had a preference for the outdoors over the indoors and would frequently take to the skies when opportunity presented itself.

Tenderly they were extracted from the crate and there was great exultation when it was discovered that they were hale and hearty and none the worse for their long journey.

The young misses had planned to take the birds to their suburban home and then, after they had familiarised themselves with the new surrounds, they would be released. It was expected that they would take speedily to their fresh environs and, in the course of time, assume the nationality of their new country. So much for the best laid schemes of doves and damsels!

In the foyer the doves were much admired but unfortunately were being passed rapidly from one pair of inexperienced hands to another so that, eventually, the inevitable happened. A *garsún* accidentally mishandled the cock of the pair. Did I say they were cock and hen? The cock grasped his chance and flew out of the open door.

There was consternation. A well-known fainter in the company promptly collapsed so that a young lady who held the second dove in her hands lost her concentration. She had also attempted to obstruct the escape of the cock and in so doing gave the French hen the opportunity she had been waiting for. With a gentle fluttering of wings she followed her companion into the sunlight which had begun to brighten the scene outside.

In a flash the crowd in the foyer had emptied itself into the square. There was no sign of the doves. Spotters were dispatched to various parts of the town and to the nearby wood of Gurtenard which was a favourite haunt of local pigeons. Although the search went on all afternoon there was no sign of the missing pair. In their absence life was obliged to go on regardless. The afternoon drifted by and when evening arrived all hope was abandoned.

After all they were innocent strangers with no knowledge of local hawks. How then could they be expected to survive!

However, an observant corner-boy whose wont it was to gaze at the sky all day spotted them on the roof of the hotel, their gleaming whiteness contrasting sublimely with the dark grey slates.

Vainly did the hotel owner, the porter, the two Ascendancy misses and numerous other well-wishers seek to lure them down from their perches. Then one Dinny Cronin appeared on the scene for the first time. Dinny was a local pigeon-fancier and was possessed of a few magnificent specimens. Indeed in those pollution-free days the sky over the dreaming town frequently played host to large flocks of pigeons. The back-yards boasted many pigeon coops and in the mornings the townspeople were frequently serenaded by soft chortlings and other manifestations of pigeonly affection.

Dinny Cronin took stock of the situation for several minutes and eventually came up with the solution.

'At home,' said he, 'I have one of the handsomest cock birds ever seen in this neck of the woods.'

On hearing that the visitors were French, Dinny was taken aback but not for long.

'My bird might have no French,' said he, 'but he has the looks and he has the carriage.'

With everybody's approval he went home for the cock and returned in jig time with the pride of his flock in his coat pocket. As cocks went he was a strapping fellow, a biller and a cooer, forceful yet demure, a winner and a wooer and a charmer of pigeons from Listowel to Knockanure. Upon beholding the French arrivals he flew upwards till he was out of sight and then tumbled crazily downwards scorning all danger in the service of courtship.

After several such amorous sallies, all calculated to win the heart of the female Frenchie, he alighted on the roof. There followed some intimate bird patter, indistinguishable to all but themselves. It was apparent that there was no language barrier.

'They speak the language of love,' said Dinny Cronin, 'and that's the same in every land under the sun.' After the tender, verbal formalities Dinny's cock bird flew off and circled the nearby Catholic church three times. The Frenchies followed suit leaving the onlookers to believe that they subscribed to the same persuasion as Dinny's cock bird.

Then the trio disappeared into the fading light and were forgotten for the moment. However, when a week went by without a sign of the vanished ménage there was widespread alarm.

In the ancient town business went on as usual but around the pigeon coops there was little billing and less cooing. Dinny Cronin's bird was sorely missed. Dinny himself was heartbroken for the missing cock was the pride of his flock.

Then a letter arrived from Paris for the young misses who had ordered the doves in the first place. The letter stated that the pair of doves had arrived back in the French capital accompanied by a dark stranger, a rude fellow with country manners but much admired by members of the opposite sex. There was widespread mourning for it was taken for granted that the Cronin cock would never leave the romantic capital of the known world and who could blame him!

Slowly but surely Christmas drew near with an abundance of freshly revealed humanity and goodwill. Dinny was disconsolate. It looked as if he would never see his pride and joy again. He sat towards the evening of Christmas Eve by the kitchen window pondering the joys of the past and the emptiness of the future.

Then his heart soared. He sat upright when he head the familiar chortle that had melted the hearts of a hundred doves. It was weak and it was hoarse but it was unmistakable. It was his missing cock bird. Dinny jumped to his feet and opened the kitchen window. There on the sill lay his friend, worn and exhausted after his journey from France and from countless other engagements too delicate to disclose and too numerous to mention.

He was received with joy and tears.

'My poor oul' cratur,' said Dinny, 'them Frenchies went near being the death of you.'

'Hush!' said his wife. 'Mustn't youth have its fling.'

Thereafter there was joy in the pigeon coops of Listowel and Dinny Cronin's prize cock wandered afar no more.

The Magic Stoolin

I was tempted for a while to call this story *A Christmas Barrel*. Everybody, I told myself, has heard of *A Christmas Carol* so why not *A Christmas Barrel*. My wife thought the title too stereotyped when I submitted it for her approval. It was then I thought of *The Magic Stoolin* and, if you care to continue, you will see why.

Times were never worse in the bogland of Booleenablawha. On the run-up to Christmas the county council had reluctantly suspended all roadwork and there was no likelihood it would resume before spring.

Of all the seven families surviving on the bog road, Jack Tobin's was the hardest hit. The others had grown-up sons and daughters working in England and America but the eldest of Jack's *cúram* was only ten and the youngest still in swaddling clothes.

There was some consolation to be drawn from the fact that there would be plenty to eat over the twelve days of Christmas. Jack had seen to that. He had disposed of ten stoolins of dry turf in the nearby town. Each stoolin was the equivalent of a clamped horse rail and each had fetched a pound in the market place. Twelve stoolins remained in the bog, impervious, because of their perfectly tapering design and solid structure, to the rain, sleet and hail which would bombard them until the advent of May.

Jack might have disposed of three or four more and thus provided himself with the wherewithal for Christmas drink but this would mean sparser fires providing the winter wind with the openings it needed to freeze the toes and chill the blood. With Jack and his wife Monnie the children always came first.

'If we pinch and pare,' Monnie had whispered as they lay on the feather bed two weeks before Christmas, 'we might rise to a dozen of stout and a half-bottle of whiskey and maybe a few minerals for the children. There's three bottles of cheap sherry left after the wake and that will do the women.'

Jack's father had expired the previous summer from nothing worse than simple senility and the subsequent wake had made massive inroads into their insubstantial savings. The couple's concern with the drink stocks did not stem in any way from their own desires for intoxicating liquor although Jack could never be charged with missing a Sunday night at the crossroads pub. Monnie would truthfully declare that drink never troubled her. The problem arose because of an age-old custom whereby each of the seven houses in Booleenablawha hosted in turn, over the Yuletide period, a modest reception for the other six.

It wasn't that the hostesses vied with each other or that drinking was excessive but it had never been known, even in the blackest of black times, that a household had run out of drink. No other hostings, apart from wakes, weddings and wren-dances, could possibly be countenanced in the hard-pressed community at any other time of year.

If the neighbours but knew of Jack's position they would have cheerfully brought a sufficiency of drink with them but this was the last thing Jack and Monnie wanted. Jack also knew that he might borrow a pound or two from a friend or that he might secure credit at the crossroads where he was known but this wasn't his way either.

The pucker would remain unsolved until the week before Christmas. The morning rain had cleared and a fresh breeze rustled in the roadside alders. Jack Tobin went among his stoolins carefully selecting the drier, darker sods for his Christmas fires. A past master in the high art of stoolin rearrangment, Jack's turf castles, as his children called them, would not disintegrate under the buffeting winds and driving rains.

As he slowly filled his ass-cart he was surprised to see the heavily laden lorry making its way over the narrow, bumpy bog-way. Jack waved at the driver and the driver waved back. Then the lorry passed by, its precious cargo of wooden porter casks swaying dangerously because of the uneven contours of the quaking road.

The man who had waved at him, Jack felt, would be a relief driver hired temporarily for the busy Christmas period who would be unfamiliar with the terrain. Otherwise he would not have departed from the main road and chosen a shorter but far more hazardous itinerary. Then it happened! There was, a hundred yards further down the road, a hump-back bridge, covered with ivy and ancient as the road itself. A cannier driver would have slowed down. As the lorry passed over, its body was suspended for a brief while when the cab dipped on the downward side. As the airborne back wheels struck the roadway a barrel leaped upward and outward and fell onto the soft margin, rolling backwards until its progress was arrested by a sally clump. Jack Tobin immediately abandoned his labours and ran towards the roadway, furiously waving and calling out at the top of his voice in a vain effort to attract the driver's attention. Then the lorry was gone. Jack Tobin found himself confronted with an untapped half-tierce of approved porter.

A half-tierce, as every wrenboy knows, contains one hundred and twenty-eight pints of dun-dark, drinkable, delight-inducing porter, porter so profuse that the drinking folk of Booleenablawha would be hard put to consume it in the round of a single night. Jack Tobin stood without moving for several minutes. There was much to be resolved. Meanwhile he would roll the barrel deeper into the sally clump lest it attract the attention of passing vagabonds and heaven knows what fate.

That night as they sat by the dying fire, with the children sound asleep in their beds, Jack informed his wife for the first time of the day's happenings and the location of the sally-girt windfall.

Monnie Tobin lifted the tongs and discovered a number of small bright coals hidden in the ashes.

After she had rearranged the fire she pointed the tongs at her spouse in order to lend emphasis to her assessment of the situation.

'First thing in the morning of Christmas Eve,' she said, 'you will cycle to town and take yourself into McFee's the wholesalers. Find out if they're missing a half-tierce of porter. If they are, the barrel will be returned. If not, we'll see.'

They spoke long into the night concerning the state of the family finances but despite all her economic wizardry, all her penny-pinching and self-sacrifice, there was no obvious way the situation could be improved.

Despite the most assiduous of searches the clerical staff at McFee's could find no record of a missing barrel. No complaint had been filed by a short-changed customer and the stock in their storehouse tallied accurately with the advice notes.

'Why?' asked the firm's charge-hand with a laugh, 'is it how you found a barrel?'

'No,' came the instant reply. 'It's just that there was a rumour going the rounds.'

Later, as night was falling on the boglands of Booleenablawha, Jack and Monnie Tobin announced to the children that they were taking a stroll. When they returned there would be a distribution of lemonade and biscuits to celebrate Christmas.

Out of doors a crisp breeze blew steadily from the south-west. Overhead a full moon shed its pale light on the rustling boglands. Now and then passing clouds obscured its rays. It proved to be an ideal night for what Jack and Monnie had in mind.

At the sally clump where lay hidden the prized half-tierce they paused and awaited one of the night's darker spells. Even then they maintained a vigil for several moments. Then when the darkness was at its most impenetrable Jack rolled the barrel from its place of concealment and, aided by his partner, pushed it slowly to where a narrow passage led on to the turf-bank where stood the twelve unassailable stoolins.

Inside the wooden cask the porter chuckled and gurgled tantalisingly. After a few moments the interior noises stopped. Jack Tobin rightly surmised that the rolling movements had brought a head to the barrel's contents. His mouth watered at the prospect of savouring the first mouthful of the cherished brew.

He had not come unprepared. In his pocket was a brass tap, a relict from numerous wakes. Earlier he had deposited a hastily hewed wooden mallet at the blind side of a specially chosen stoolin. The mallet would serve nicely to drive the tap home when the barrel was in place. Jack had the additional foresight to bring along a brace and bit together with a tapering wooden spike which would be used to plug the bung-hole made by the former in order to facilitate an expeditious flow from the tap.

Jack's special skills and foresight with regard to regulating the condition and the drawing of porter came from long experience. In addition to the annual wren-dances which flourished throughout the region there were countless wakes where several porter barrels might be on flow at the same time. Consequently there were few houses in the countryside without some sort of porter tap and a brace and bit.

As in all trades there were the highly skilled and the botchers. With so much hinging on a successful outcome it would have been unthinkable to entrust the tapping of a full barrel containing such an irreplaceable commodity to an incompetent! Only the practised and the proven were elected to take charge of such a momentous undertaking. Jack Tobin was one of these.

On their arrival at the stoolin he quickly removed two-thirds of the upper body. Then with a mighty effort he lifted the half-tierce and laid it horizontally on the carefully structured base. Without hurry he bedded it firmly, but lovingly, so that it would lie still during the tapping. One, two, three rapid, accurate, beautifully timed strokes and the tap was firmly embedded in the barrel.

Without undue haste Jack Tobin remade the stoolin all around the recumbent cask. The demands of this difficult task brought out the artist in him. True, he was aided by a full moon but it is the touch as much as the perception that makes the difference between a great stoolin-maker and an indifferent one.

Smearing a liberal handful of turf mould over the exposed tap he extracted a tin pannikin from his coat pocket. Now would come the acid test. Those in the countryside who were partial to porter, and they were many, would quite rightly aver that every content of every barrel tasted differently. Some were too highly conditioned and some were too flat. Some carried a bitter tang whilst, worst of all, others were casky and decidedly unpalatable. Casky barrels were rare and were always replaced by the brewing house. Unfortunately, because of the nature of its acquisition, no such redress would be available to Jack Tobin if the lost barrel was tainted.

He looked upward first at his heavenly ally, still free of cloud and undisputed queen of the heavens. What if the barrel was filled with water or with cleansing fluid! Holding the pannikin under the spout he turned on the tap. A powerful jet of sweetly smelling porter foam knocked the pannikin from his hand. Quickly he turned off the tap and reclaimed the pannikin.

At his second attempt he only partially turned on the tap. The diminished outflow, still powerful, smote merrily against the bottom of the pannikin so that Jack was obliged to slant the shallow vessel in order to avoid a spillage. When the pannikin was filled he allowed it to rest atop the stoolin so that the froth might subside and the porter proper accumulate beneath. When he judged the time to be ripe he handed the pannikin to his wife. First she tasted and then, delighted by the first impressions, swallowed heartily, declaring when the pannikin was drained that she had never tasted the likes in all her days.

'It's like cream,' she announced, wiping her lips, 'only nicer.'

After several pannikins each they recovered their possessions and, hand in hand, returned homewards, their happy way benignly lighted by the liberal moon.

'Did you ever taste the likes of it?' Monnie Tobin asked as they neared home.

'Never!' Jack assented as he squeezed her hand and placed a frothy kiss on her upturned lips, frothy too. That night, full of porter-induced, seasonal mansuetude, Jack and Monnie Tobin sang the gentle songs of their youth for their delighted children.

Time passed until all that remained of the twelve days of Christmas were two. It was the night the Tobins played host to their neighbours all. Never was there such a night. Every half-hour or so Jack Tobin would disappear, through his back door, bearing two small milking buckets. In a matter of minutes he would be back again with two buckets brim-full of the most nourishing, the most savoury, the most flavoursome porter ever consumed in that part of the world, or so the neighbours said.

Naturally they questioned its origin when it

loosened their tongues. Jack informed them that it had come from the city of Limerick through the good offices of a calf jobber who was partially indebted to him for having extended credit to him earlier in the year.

And how had he transported it was the next question tabled? Oh by milk churn of course and had not Jack carefully transferred it from the jobber's churn to his own where it had, slowly but surely, acquired the immaculate condition which set it apart from the less exhilarating porter of former years! More evidence, however, was required by the discerning elders of Booleenablawha and, indeed, more evidence was forthcoming.

'And pray!' asked Jack's immediate neighbour, a man with an insatiable appetite for information, regardless of its veracity, 'could you tell us the name of the tavern where this porter was purchased?'

The question caught Jack unawares. There was also the lamentable fact that he did not know the name of a solitary tavern in the city of Limerick for the good reason that he had never been there.

'The name of the tavern you say!' He pretended to ponder.

It was his wife who came to his aid. 'The name

of the tavern,' said Monnie Tobin, without batting an eyelid, 'is the Magic Stoolin.'

'The Magic Stoolin!' the neighbour repeated, 'sure don't I know well where it is.'

The last thing the poor fellow wanted to profess was ignorance of this well-known watering place which was surely known to man, woman and child in the city of Limerick and other places besides.

As it turned out the Magic Stoolin was known to several other accomplished liars in the gathering who had never been to Limerick either and also to their womenfolk who were in the habit of supporting them, without question, in all manner of spurious claims and submissions over the years.

From such unfailing corroborations are lasting marriages nurtured, are peace and probity maintained within the family and are Christmases revered and relished in the simple homesteads of Booleenablawha.

The Great Christmas

Raid at Ballybooley

It all happened back in 1920 when those heinous wretches known as the Black and Tans were hell-bent on maiming, murdering and all forms of diabolical destruction and showing themselves to be true credits to the calabooses from which they had been released in order to serve their country and shoot innocent Irish people.

No day passed without some skirmish or other between the dreaded invaders and the brave boys of the North Kerry Flying Column. The more notable of these encounters are suitably remembered in song and story but none more so than the great Christmas raid at Ballybooley. True, this singular event has its controversial side but in this respect it must be said that no two accounts of any battle are similar in every detail.

The year in question produced one of the driest summers ever recorded. The hills, in fact, turned brown. On the turf banks the sods dried of their own accord which was a blessing indeed to youthful turf-turners and stoolin-makers who were free to spend the long summer days by river and stream or lazing in carefree groups in woodland and meadow.

Nobody, however, can put forward the claim that Mother Nature spreads her output indiscriminately and as though to prove this point beyond doubt she presented the North Kerry countryside with a succeeding Christmas of unprecedented bitterness and savagery.

Hail, rain and snow were commonplace whilst, in between, Jack Frost worked overtime. The tinder-dry turf of the summer made no battle in the gusty hearths of cottage and farmhouse and people were wont to say, not for the first time, that if there was anything worse than turf that was too wet then surely it was turf that was too dry. Many of the roadside reeks were consumed before Christmas. Rusty saws and axes were resurrected for the felling of timber. Fuel theft grew rife as the winter wore on.

In all the bogland area perhaps the most practised lifter of the unguarded sod was a man by the name of Micky Dooley. He was well known to all and sundry as a professional turf thief. All through November and December when the moon shone fitfully, if at all, he would betake himself with ass and rail to a convenient bog, there to ply his shifty trade.

Under cover of darkness he would fill his rail from ill-made reeks whose appearances would not be affected by the disappearance of an ass-rail of turf. It was different with well-made reeks. A solitary sod out of place and the owner was immediately alerted.

A well-made reek was a match for anything be it thunder, gale or turf thief. Each sod was so close to the next and each corner so smoothed and well constructed that even the absence of a single cadhrawn would be easily detected. Consequently turf thieves shied away from well-made structures and concentrated on the badly-made, misshapen ones. It was to these latter on the dark and stormy nights around Christmas that Micky Dooley directed his ass and cart. His target, of course, would have been thoroughly reconnoitred beforehand. One might see him sauntering casually in the distance, his head averted from roadside reeks, his gaze fixed steadfastly in front of him as though reek-rape was the farthest thought from his mind. Yet without once inclining his head or slowing his gait he absorbed every detail of his night-time objective.

His attention might seem to be fixed on a flock of wheeling plover in the skies overhead or rapt in admiration at a particular rampart of cloud but all the while he stored detail after vital detail for future reference.

He would have to discover in the little time available to him if there was room for donkey and cart at the bogland side of the reek or if the reek had already been gutted by storm and above all to determine the quality of the turf. It was essential that it resemble in texture, size and shape the inadequate supply he had harvested for his own use in case a suspicious reek owner decided to investigate.

When his rail was filled he would skilfully rearrange the area which he had plundered so that it was always next to impossible to detect the loss. This was an art in itself. His efforts were always constricted by the absence of light. As a result he worked like a man demented whenever a ray of moonlight filtered through the flying clouds. Moonlight is the natural enemy of the night-raider but he needs a little now and then to be going on with.

Largely, however, Micky worked by the feel, waiting for a token of moonlight to add the finishing touches. He never took more than one rail from any reek and this was the real secret of his success. Suspect he might be but there was no proof and so long as he confined his looting to reasonable quantities his thieving excursions were taken for granted.

Those whose reeks escaped molestation were fond of saying it was a poor bog indeed that couldn't support a solitary turf thief.

Then came a fearful night shortly before Christmas. The north-eastern gales bore down the sky furiously whipping and flailing the already tormented countryside. Sitting by his fire Micky decided that it was an excellent night for an enterprising fellow like himself. Reluctant though he was to forsake his warm hearth the night was heaven-sent for his purpose.

Nobody in his right mind, a turf-thief apart, would venture abroad under such conditions and who was to say but the weather might take a dramatic turn for the better and so curtail his outdoor activities when they might most be needed. He resolved to venture forth.

He tackled the unwilling donkey to the ancient cart, assembled the rail thereon and, to ensure silence, liberally plastered the axle screw-nuts with car grease. He bound himself thoroughly against the elements and set forth on his journey.

A worse night he had never experienced. Within minutes his gloved hands were freezing, the fingers stripped of circulation. He closed his eyes against the storm and blindly followed the donkey. He would have turned back after the first quarter mile but he reminded himself sensibly that after a storm comes a calm and since his turf stocks were almost exhausted he simply had to make the most of his opportunity.

Slowly, patiently, man and beast battled against the savage blasts until both were on the threshold of exhaustion. At length they arrived at the bog lane where the several remaining reeks stood awaiting the inevitable. As they reached the first of these, one which he had rifled a bare fortnight before, the donkey stopped dead and despite all Micky's urgings refused to proceed against the gale-force wind. Micky knew that the poor animal had reached the end of its tether. There was nothing for it but to turn round and proceed homewards. At least they would have the wind behind them. He backed the donkey into the lee of the reek. There it would regain its wind for the return journey. As he waited, in the bitter cold, the combination of temptation and habit proved too much for Micky Dooley.

'All I'll take is a few sods,' he told himself, 'for since I have raided this reek before, to take any more would be folly.'

Alas his rapacious instincts prevailed and in no time at all he had the rail filled and clamped.

The days passed with no abatement in the weather. Soon the rightful owner of the turf put in an appearance with a horse and cart and proceeded to fill his rail. The first thing he noticed, upon his arrival, was a sizable declivity at the reek's rear. A grim smile appeared on his weather-beaten face. This merely proved to be the prelude to the heartiest of laughs and, this in turn was followed by a gleeful shout and a rubbing together of the palms of the hands.

For several moments he cavorted delightedly around the roadway. For long he had suspected Micky Dooley. He estimated that over the years the turf thief had relieved him of twenty ass-rails at the very least. When, a few weeks before, he visited the reek his suspicions had been aroused upon beholding a small mound of fresh donkey dung close by the reek. A sure sign, this, that a donkey had dallied there.

Carefully he had inspected the reek but could find no sign of interference. This did not surprise him in the least as it was not Micky Dooley's wont to leave evidence of his visits.

The proprietor of the reek was forced to concede that Micky was without peer in the art of restructuring turf reeks. He would have dearly loved to lay hands on him there and then if for no other purpose than to strangle him.

As he filled his rail he considered ways and means of snaring the thief. Suddenly an inspired albeit murderous notion struck him. Frequently he played host to men on the run and sometimes they concealed their guns and ammunition on his property. That night he revisited his reek, his pockets filled with live ammunition. With the utmost care he inserted a score of bullets in the softer of those sods which occupied the weakest corner of the reek. Now a fortnight later he congratulated himself on his foresight. He had gambled that the thief would pay a second visit because of the severity of the weather and he had won. That night in bed he conveyed the tidings to his wife.

'I have prepared,' he said, 'a terrific Christmas gift for Micky Dooley. It's a gift he'll never forget till the day he dies and I have to say that no man deserves it more.'

He then told her about the live ammunition embedded in the sods.

'Oh sweet Mary Immaculate,' his wife cried out clutching her rosary beads, 'suppose someone is struck by a bullet.'

'I don't care,' said her husband, 'if the hoor is blown to Kingdom Come. He'll never steal another sod from me one way or the other.'

Chuckling to himself he turned over on his side and slept the sleep of the just. His wife prayed into the small hours faithfully accompanied by the sonorous snores of her husband. She beseeched every saint with every prayer in her repertoire that no harm would befall the household of Micky Dooley.

Less than a week later, on Christmas Eve to be exact, Micky was seated in front of a roaring fire with his wife and children and a neighbour who had called to exchange titbits of gossip in return for basking cold shins before the glowing sods. Outside the wind howled and hissed whilst hordes of unruly hailstones hopped and danced on road and roof.

'God bless us,' said the female neighbour, by name Maggie Mulloy, 'isn't a good fire the finest thing of all.'

'True for you Maggie,' her host responded. 'I wouldn't swap a good fire for a bottle of whiskey.'

There they sat, happily contemplating the leaping flames, savouring the warmth and comfort of the hearthside. A happier scene could not be imagined. A black buck cat, fat and sleek, sat at his master's feet while the children intoned their rhymes in a drowsy hum that added to the somnolent atmosphere of the fireside scene.

'Thanks be to God for a turf fire,' Maggie Mulloy said under her breath and then in a louder tone, 'and thanks to them that has the heart and the nature to share that same.'

Micky accepted the compliment as befitted such a magnanimous benefactor.

'Tut-tut,' he said dismissively, 'tut-tut.'

The cat purred, the women nodded and Micky reached forward a foot to restore a wayward sod which had fallen too far from the fire. The sparks shot upwards in a bright display which boasted every conceivable shade of red. Then suddenly all hell broke loose. The first bullet smashed into the paraffin lamp which hung by a chain from a central rafter between two flitches of yellowing bacon. There followed immediately a minor explosion after which the light went out.

The second bullet smashed into the dresser and shook it to its foundations as well as sending saucers, cups and ware of all sorts flying about the kitchen. The third bullet went straight between the two eyes of the cat. Without as much as a mew he stiffened and expired where he lay, a taunting parody of the nine lives supposed to be his right.

For several seconds after the first shot Micky Dooley remained rooted to his chair, unable to move. His mouth opened and closed but no sound emanated therefrom. He was shocked to his very core. A bullet whistling past his ear brought a sudden end to his inactivity. Ignoring the cries of the women and children he bolted for the bedroom where he barricaded the door behind him and dived straightaway under the bed.

He shut out the appalling din in the kitchen by the simple expedient of thrusting a finger into either ear. His heart raced so violently that he feared for its continued beating. No heart, he felt, could continue at such a pace without coming to a sudden and untimely halt. Trembling, he invoked the aid of his dead mother after which he loudly beseeched the Sacred Heart to succour him in his final agony.

In the kitchen there was absolute bedlam. The screams were deafening. Neighbours, near and far, were brought to their doors by the mixture of shots and cries of human torment.

"Tis the Black and Tans,' one terrified listener called out. 'There's a battle on in Ballybooley.'

His cry was quickly taken up and in jig time every door and window in the district was barricaded. Lights were doused and Rosaries recited. Holy water was sprinkled here, there and everywhere.

Meanwhile back at the Dooley kitchen three more bullets went off. The first of these passed through the window. The other two ricocheted up the chimney and spent themselves harmlessly on the night air. Mercifully none of the kitchen's occupants was injured. A sustained silence ensued but a longer period was to pass before Micky Dooley opened the bedroom door. At that precise moment the last bullet exploded from the fire and pierced the upper of his left boot. It lodged in his instep. He fell to the floor, a cry of anguish on his lips.

'They got me,' he screamed.

His wife and children knelt by his side while Maggie Mulloy breathed an Act of Contrition into his ear. After a while, when it was clear that the shooting had ended, they lifted him onto a chair where he sat with the injured leg resting on another chair. Maggie, who lived less than a stone's throw away, had gone and returned in a thrice with a noggin of whiskey. Micky disposed of it without assistance. The eldest of the children was dispatched to a neighbour's house with the curt instructions that a doctor and priest were to be contacted at once.

Outside the wind had abated and soon neighbours from every house within a two-mile radius converged upon the house. The same question formed on the lips of every last one of them. What had happened?

'We were ambushed,' Micky Dooley explained.

'But why?' the communal question came.

The wounded man shook his head knowingly and brought a silencing finger to his lips indicating that there was more involved here than met the eye.

'We were ambushed,' he exclaimed to every newcomer.

'By whom?' the question came automatically on the heels of the others.

'Tans,' was Micky's immediate response. He kept repeating the word embellishing it every so often with choice adjectives. Eventually and inevitably the man who had planted the bullets arrived upon the scene. Tentatively he thrust his head inside the door.

'Black and Tans,' Micky disembarrassed him before he had a chance to apologise and spoil the entire proceedings. The bullet-planter nodded vigorously, relieved beyond measure that no one had been killed. As it was, if the truth were to become known, the least for which he would be held accountable would be attempted murder.

'Tans it was,' he confirmed. 'Didn't I see them with my own two eyes and they making off down the road.'

Micky Dooley bent his head in gratitude and relief. It was only then that he noticed the dead cat. He lifted the stiffening form to his lips and kissed it on top of the head which was a change indeed for the only other part of the creature's anatomy with which he had any previous contact was its posterior whenever he applied one of his hobnailed boots to that sensitive area for no reason whatsoever.

'My poor cat,' he called out while his eyes calefacted huge tears to suit the occasion. One by one the neighbours departed, arguing heatedly as to why such a savage attack had been made on a household which had no apparent connection with the Freedom Fighters.

They came to the only conclusions possible. The Tans had been seen by a reliable witness. They were, therefore, responsible for the attack. They would not have carried out the attack unless Micky Dooley was a dispatch carrier or was in the habit of secretly harbouring the men on the run.

Apart from Micky only one man knew the truth and that man's lips were sealed. It was that or subject himself to the possibility of a stiff prison sentence. There was no point in taking such a gamble. One thing was certain. Micky Dooley would never interfere with one of his reeks again. Others yes but not his. That had been the primary point of the exercise.

Time passed and word of the raid spread. The account was handsomely embroidered with the passage of the years so that, in the end, it transpired that Micky had single-handed, armed only with a double-barrelled shotgun, routed a score of Black and Tans killing none but wounding several while he himself would be a martyr to a pronounced limp for the remainder of his life. His neighbour Maggie Mulloy came to be revered throughout the countryside. Had she not fought by her neighbour's side? None begrudged her the paltry state pension and service medals which a grateful government had conferred on all those who had participated in the Fight for Freedom.

Micky Dooley fared better. Because of his limp he was awarded, in addition to his service pension, a handsome disability allowance which left him secure for the remainder of his days.

Maggie Mulloy eventually came to believe her own story. Without doubt, on a gusty winter's night under a fitful moon, shadows may be easily transformed into human shapes. No great effort is afterwards required to deck them in uniforms. Far from abandoning his old ways Micky Dooley redoubled his raids upon vulnerable turf ricks. Now he stole with impunity. Wasn't it his right he told himself. Didn't he single-handed defeat a company of Black and Tans! By God if he wasn't entitled to a few sods of somebody else's turf who was! Wasn't he one of the two surviving heroes of the Battle of Ballybooley. The bullet-planter would never mention the Christmas gift again, not even to this wife.

From time to time strangers visited Mickey Dooley's house to inspect the holes left by the bullets and to view the almost fatal wound upon his instep. Veneration was also paid to the memory of the cat whose life was ended so tragically in the service of its master. As Micky Dooley used to say when reminded of the creature's demise: 'Greater love no cat hath than the cat who lays down his life for his friends.'

Cider

I forget my exact age during the Christmas in question but I must have been at least seventeen for, dare I say it gentle reader, I was greatly addicted to cider and foolishly believed that I could drink any amount of it. Addicted though I was I drank it but rarely and always discreetly. My father had his suspicions but he never caught me in the act and always I made sure to steal into bed when I was intoxicated. With companions of my own age I would indulge in secret sessions on certain feast days and holy days about five times a year in all and once at Christmas. That would have been the Christmas I saw and heard the banshee.

The banshee was heard only when a person with an O or a Mac in the surname passed away. Originally my family were O'Kanes and none was surer than myself that this plaintive and panic-inducing apparition would not be duped by the minor deviation in name.

I had heard the banshee in the past. We would be sitting by the fire late at night, my mother darning socks, my father reading the newspaper of the day and we, the children, readying ourselves for bed.

'Hush!' my mother would suddenly raise a hand for absolute silence. In moments the requisite hush would have descended and then, fully alerted, we would wait for the inevitable with looks of alarm on our faces. From afar would come the supernatural wailing, spine-chilling and pitiful, not belonging to this world. My mother would make the sign of the cross while we all followed suit except my father.

'Another poor soul on its way to the great beyond,' my mother would whisper.

'Another sex-starved greyhound,' my father would announce with a good-humoured shake of his head.

Time rolled on and the family grew. One month I would be five feet six and by the end of the following month I would be five feet seven. It was growing time. By the time Christmas arrived I was five feet ten inches and rapidly heading for six feet.

It had been agreed that my father, my mother and the girls would assemble in the kitchen at eleven-thirty so that all would be in time for midnight mass at the church of St Mary's. Earlier we had partaken of lemonade and biscuits in honour of the season. After the turkey had been trussed and stuffed in readiness for Christmas Day my father was declared exempt from further involvement in the household chores. He headed at once for the neighbourhood pub where most of his cronies would already have ensconced themselves. For days before I had strenuously argued that I had grown too old to be a part of the familistic excursion to the church reminding my parents of my great age and height and pointing out that all my friends had received permission to attend mass on their own or with their chosen companions.

My sisters took my part but my father was adamant saying it had come to his ears that the teenagers of the parish were more interested in cider and porter than in the pursuance of their Christmas duties. In the end he relented but only when my mother forcibly reminded him that he had been young himself.

'Very well so,' I remember his words well as he clasped his hands behind his back, 'but if it comes to my attention that you place the consumption of cider before the fulfilment of your religious duties I will confine you to your room for twenty-four hours, without recourse to appeal, and in addition I will kick your posterior so hard that your front teeth will fall out as a result.'

'Cider!' I spat out the word disdainfully as though it were the last thought in my head.

Two hours before midnight I slipped out of the house by the back door and joined my friends in Moorey's public house. The only light in the tiny bar was from a flickering candle. The limbs of the law were abroad on public house duty and Moorey spoke in whispers.

'Happy Christmas!' he said and handed me a pint of cider on the house.

Moorey was old as the hills, grey as a slate, ribald, randy and irreligious but he was a generous soul and no other publican in town would serve us for fear of reprisals from parents and the custodians of the peace. Despite this my mother and the other matrons of the street liked him. They had known his late wife. He had apparently loved her dearly and had always shown it in his treatment of her while she was alive. He had not remarried although she had been dead for thirty years. Every Sunday he would place fresh flowers on her grave.

Like ourselves he was addicted to cider with the difference that he would lace his pints with dollops of whiskey and yet we never saw him drunk.

Sometimes there would be the barest suggestion of a lurch but nothing remotely resembling the phenomenal staggers executed by seemingly indestructible drunkards when the pubs were closed for the night.

While we sat quietly drinking pint after pint of cider we spoke for the most part about girls, sometimes maliciously and sometimes boastfully which is the way of youth.

As the midnight hour drew near we could hear the hurrying footsteps outside the window as young and old made their way to midnight mass. As if by common consent there was no conversation, no laughter, none of the raucous cries one associates with crowds or noisy clatter of boots and shoes. Such was the love and respect for the celebratory season that unnecessary noises were regarded in the same light as profanities.

At ten minutes to twelve Moorey announced that it was time to go. At such an hour, on any other night of the year, the session would only be starting but as Moorey explained gently: 'Because of the night that's in it boys I think it's time to douse the candle.'

We finished our pints in the pitch dark

promising to meet again on St Stephen's night. In turn we shook hands with Moorey and extended to him the compliments of season. Outside on the street only the stragglers remained.

We had earlier decided against mass for a number of reasons; if our parents saw us they would immediately recognise our state of intoxication. Then there was the possibility that one or more of us would be nauseated by the heat of the church and the burning incense, which could well bring on a fit of vomiting. Then there was the most important factor of all and that was the likelihood that one or more of us would be obliged to lessen the strain on brimming bladders and to do this it would be necessary to stand up in the full view of the congregation and make one's way to the end of one's pew and thence up the long aisle under the suspicious stares of friends, neighbours, parents and strangers. Many would smirk knowingly, aware of our plight and destination, which would of necessity be the convenient back wall of the holy sanctuary which was attached to the rear of the church. Our parents, of course, would be infuriated, knowing full well that we would have to be truly cider-smitten to run such a gauntlet!

We went our separate ways with none of the boisterous farewells in which we would indulge on less devotional occasions. At home the kitchen was strangely silent. On the mantelpiece the clock, unheard throughout the day, was having its full say at last. A burned-out turf sod crumbled softly into the overflowing ash-pan of the Stanley Number 8.

I suddenly felt a profound longing for the girls and for my parents. Supposing they never came back! I dismissed the terrible thought and counted the twelve intrusions which introduced the midnight hour. The final chime extended itself to the ultimate limits where silence lay waiting to receive its spirit. Then, from the rear of the house, came a long, low, wailing sound which made the hairs stand to attention on that area of the head nearest to my forehead. I had known these hairs all my life and I can swear that they never behaved in such a fashion before. While I waited for them to resume their normal stance there came, stealing through the partly opened back door of the kitchen, the same wailing sound. My hairs remained alert while my heart raced and my whole frame shivered. Suddenly I grew less tense. This new state was no doubt induced by a mixture of cider and youthful bravado!

The wailing started again, this time more protracted and pitiful, as though the soul of the voice box from which it originated had been recently drowned in the unfathomable depths of black despair.

Again my heart raced and the hairs already standing were joined by their brethren from every quarter of the head. Such was their consistency that they would have served as a bed of nails for a novice fakir. Only the wailing of the banshee could stiffen human hairs to such a degree.

Then, for the first time in my entire life, my knees knocked and I was obliged to place my hands on the table for support. There came almost immediately a sustained high-pitched pillalooing of such intensity that I was obliged to stuff my fingers in my ears lest my hearing be permanently damaged. It was as though the ghostly proprietress of such unearthly vocal organs was endeavouring to reach notes never attained before. Their pitch seemed to far exceed the range of the most accomplished soprano and then, unexpectedly, came a collapsing and a crumbling followed by a mixture of base trebles and last of all by the most musical grunts and groans imaginable as though the banshee in question was about to give birth.

Emboldened by the cider I cautiously made my way into our back yard. The sickle moon shone fitfully, its pale glow frequently impaired by heedless clouds. Slowly I advanced towards the back door of the out-house where the winter's supply of turf was stored.

I had frequently heard of the silence of the grave when older folk spoke reverently of the dead and such indeed was the silence of the out-house at that point in time on that unforgettable night. I was not prepared for what happened next. I was standing close to the rickety door straining my ears for tell-tale sounds when I head the uneven breathing of some creature in the immediate vicinity of the door's exterior. On second thoughts, panting might be a more apt word. Then came a horrifying caterwauling as terrifying as it was unexpected. It exploded right into my ear which was pressed against the door. I was paralysed, my feet like hundred-weights of lead, my heart thumping as though, at any minute, it would burst through the walls of my chest. I would have taken off that instant but my legs refused to budge. I was tied down by my own terror. I prayed silently to the Blessed Virgin.

'Mother of the Sacred Jesus,' I whispered imploringly, 'come to my aid this night.'

Suddenly my natural courage, scant as it was, surfaced and with a mighty roar I opened the door. The creature tumbled in on top of me and we both fell in a heap astride the turf sods scattered around the floor. She persisted with her lamentations as she lay on the ground writhing and kicking out in torment.

It was as much as I could do to get to my feet. When I did I fell a second time on top of the black-shawled creature from the spirit world. I had accidentally stood on a turf sod which spun beneath my foot, capsizing me. This time I rolled over on my side in a desperate effort to escape the clutches of the hideous creature with the overpowering smell.

At that moment a wayward moon shaft entered the out-house through its only window and highlighted the features of the awful apparition which would surely tear my eyes out if she could but lay her filthy talons on me.

The moon shaft rested for a moment on the bloodshot eyes before drifting downwards to the almost toothless mouth, redeemed from emptiness by the presence of a solitary black fang from which venom dripped as she tried in vain to smite me.

In anguish I cried out to the heavens for help and the heavens in their mercy answered. I dived through the out-house window and into the back yard where my head struck a stone so that I was rendered half unconscious.

Fuming and screaming and uttering unmentionable maledictions she towered over me. A number of small bones materialised in her grimy paws. These she flung at me with all her might but most whizzed harmlessly by. One struck me just above the eye. There was no doubt about its origin. It was a human finger bone as were the others which lay scattered about the back yard.

I managed to crawl away from her towards the door of the kitchen. Curiously she made no attempt to follow me. On all fours, like a wounded animal, I made for the sanctuary of the kitchen.

I bolted the door behind me and ran up the stairs to bed where I pulled the clothes over my head without disrobing. I lay there shaking and moaning, beseeching the Blessed Mother of God to succour and comfort me.

After a while I slunk from the bed to the window which commanded a full view of the back yard and out-house. The moon had just unloaded a cargo of ghastly light. There was no sign of the banshee.

Making the Sign of the Cross I returned to my bed and promptly fell asleep. No doubt the shock of the night's happenings played a part in my sudden collapse into deep slumber. The next sound I heard was my mother's voice calling me in the half light of the morning.

'Hurry!' she was saying, 'and you'll just be on time for ten o'clock mass.'

I lay on my bed fervently wishing that I had not consumed so much of Moorey's cider. It was only then that the awful happenings of the night came flooding back. I hurried downstairs. My father sat at the head of the table smoking his pipe. He threw me a withering look before the commencement of his interrogation.

Before he had time to pose a single question I blurted out my story. Horrified, my poor mother clutched her bosom and flopped into the chair which my father had instantly provided lest she fall on the floor. As I revealed the full details of my horrific encounter my mother's face grew paler and paler. My father puffed upon his pipe at a furious rate. There was a cloud of blue smoke underhanging the ceiling by the time I finished.

'The banshee you say!' My father emptied the bowl of his pipe into the ash-pan of the Stanley.

'Without question,' I replied as we both waited for my mother to stop shaking her head. The shaking was accompanied by the most holy of spiritual aspirations, all directed upwards in thanksgiving for my salvation.

My father sighed deeply which meant that he was also thinking deeply. Without another word he filled his pipe while I waited for his verdict. There was none forthcoming. Instead he rose without a word and went into the back yard where he spent a considerable time. When he returned his hands were clasped behind his back.

'You say,' he opened, 'that the bones she flung at you were finger bones!'

'Yes,' came my ready answer.

'Human fingers?'

'Yes.'

He took his right hand from behind his back and threw a fistful of small bones on the table.

'These,' he announced solemnly, 'are the very bones which lay scattered around the yard just now. Will you confirm that these are the bones which were flung at you last night by the banshee?'

'There's no doubt in my mind,' I replied.

Guardedly I fingered the bones which still retained some tissue and a residue of meat. It was clear that they had been well and truly gnawed.

'And you say they are human?' My father was now at his most inquisitorial. All the family knew that he secretly fancied himself as a prosecutor. He was always at the head and tail of every domestic investigation, strutting around the kitchen with his hands clasped behind his back, taking them apart occasionally and joining them together at the uppermost point of his paunch as he listened to evidence and submissions.

Sometimes he would close his eyes as he questioned a hostile witness. Other times he would stand silently for long periods, his eyes firmly fixed upon the defendant who was generally myself. This tactic nearly always worked with the girls who would readily confess to anything, just to be free of his accusing eye. I must say that the entire household enjoyed such trials at the end of which everybody, except yours truly, was acquitted and exonerated. When convicted I would be confined to my bedroom for periods of one hour to a maximum of four although the possibility of a twenty-four-hour sentence was always on the cards.

'My Lord!' he unexpectedly addressed himself to my mother who had sufficiently recovered her composure to acknowledge the surprise judicial appointment, 'these bones you see before you which the defendant claims are human finger bones are nothing of the sort. They are, in fact, bones from a pig's foot or *crubín* which is the local term affectionately applied to this particular extension of the pig's anatomy.'

My mother rose to examine the evidence, nodded her head in agreement and resumed her seat.

'Not only is the defendant a pathological liar,' my father was continuing, 'but he is a deceitful scoundrel as well.'

'Please proceed!' was all my mother said.

My father cleared his throat.

'You are aware,' said he, 'of the existence of a woman known as Madgeen Buggerworth?'

'Yes!' I replied with a laugh.

'You will respect the court sir!' my father cautioned, 'or you'll be fined for contempt.'

I bent my head submissively and tried to look

contrite. This wasn't easy, for the very mention of Madgeen Buggerworth's name was enough to make anyone laugh. She was a local beggar-woman and it was frequently said of her that she never drew a sober breath. On reflection it would be true to say that I had never seen her sober.

Madgeen was a powerful virago of a woman. Her husband had died after siring the final member of her thirteen-strong family and the family, the moment they were fledged, took off for foreign parts and were never seen again and small blame to them because she was never done with scolding and beating them.

Her favourite pose was when she spread her legs apart in the middle of the roadway and threw off the black shawl which truly covered multitudes. Up then would go the front of her skirts so that her bare midriff was exposed to the world. Then would come the drunken boast as she touched her navel with the index finger of her right hand: 'There now,' she would call out at the top of her voice for all to hear, 'there now is a belly that never reared a bastard!'

She would rant and rave, skirts aloft until the civic guards came on the scene and ushered her homewards. Other times she was to be seen lying in one of the town's laneways with her back to a wall, fast asleep, snoring in drunken abandon. Given enough drink she could sleep anywhere, regardless of wind or rain. She was to be seen too late at night staggering from one doorway to another singing at the top of her voice, if singing it could be called.

'If it please the court I would request that your worship and the defendant follow me to the out-house where I shall provide incontrovertible evidence that this man,' my father pointed a finger in my direction, 'was so bereft of sense from the consumption of cider that he confused our friend Madgeen Buggerworth with the banshee.'

He led the way into the back yard and on to the out-house where we were greeted by deep snoring punctuated now and then by outbreaks of spluttering and wheezing. There on the ground, partly covered by turf sods, lay Madgeen Buggerworth. By her side there lay an uneaten *crubín*.

'We'll let her sleep for the present,' my father announced, 'later,' again he pointed in my direction, 'when she wakes you will serve her with dinner and afterwards you will take her home.'

I hoped that this would be his last word on the

matter but there was more to follow.

'Let us return to the kitchen,' he said solemnly, 'where your sentence will be handed down. Meanwhile I suggest you pray for mercy.'

So saying he preceded us into the kitchen where he announced that he was relieving my mother of all judicial responsibilities on the grounds that she would be incapable because of her known affection for the defendant of meting out a just sentence.

I stood with my back to the Stanley awaiting the pleasure of the court. My father stood at the doorway, hands clasped behind back. My mother sat in a neutral corner.

'I find you guilty of drunkenness in the first degree,' he said, 'and I hereby sentence you to twenty-four hours' solitary confinement in your room.'

I stood aghast! It was the toughest sentence he had ever handed down. I would have to admit that I expected no less. He was clearing his throat again.

'There are, however,' he proceeded solemnly, 'mitigating circumstances. This day as you know is the birthday of a great and good man who was once wrongly convicted and subsequently crucified. As a small measure of atonement for that woeful miscarriage of justice I hereby suspend the sentence imposed upon you. You are, therefore, entitled to walk from this court a free man.'

On my way home from mass I met him walking down the street against me. It had turned unexpectedly into the mildest of days.

'Let's have a stroll before dinner,' he suggested.

We took the pathway to the river which was in modest flood. He spoke about other Christmases, of his father and grandfather and of great wobbling geese especially stall fed for the Christmas dinner, of whiskey drinking, great-uncles and carol singing and the innocent pranks of his youth. We walked through the oak wood, marvelling at the splendid contributions of the songbirds despite the greyness of the day and the leafless trees and hedgerows.

We re-entered the town at the end farthest from where we left it and proceeded down the long thoroughfare known as Church Street. We turned off into a laneway and found ourselves at the rear door of Moorey's premises. I was astonished to discover that my father was familiar with the sesame of admission, two knocks and a pause, two knocks a pause and finally three knocks. The door opened after a short wait and Moorey stood there, surprise showing on his face.

'Long time no see, Master!' he said with a smile.

Inside we sat on stools at the bar counter.

'Do you think this man has graduated from cider Moorey?' my father asked.

Moorey considered the question carefully before answering. Then after a while he said: 'Just about.'

'Then,' said my father as he laid a hand on my shoulder, 'we'll have two pints of stout to sharpen the appetite.'

Many Years Ago

Many years ago, in our street, there lived an old woman who had but one son whose name was Jack. Jack's father had died when Jack was no more than a *garsún* but Jack's mother went out to work to support her son and herself.

As Jack grew older she still went out and worked for the good reason that Jack did not like work. The people in the street used to say that Jack was only good for three things. He was good for eating, he was good for smoking and he was good for drinking. Now to give him his due he never beat his mother or abused her verbally. All he did was to skedaddle to England when she was too old to go out to work. Years passed but she never had a line from her only son. Every Christmas she would stand inside her window waiting for a card or a letter. She waited in vain.

When Christmas came to our street it came with a loud laugh and an expansive humour that healed old wounds and lifted the hearts of young and old. If the Christmas that came to our street were a person he would be something like this:

he would be in his sixties but glowing with rude health. His face would be flushed and chubby with sideburns down to the rims of his jaws. He would be wearing gaiters and a bright tweed suit and he would be mildly intoxicated. His pockets would be filled with silver coins for small boys and girls and for the older folk he would have a party at which he would preside with his waist-coated paunch extending benignly and his posterior benefiting from the glow of a roaring log fire.

There would be scalding punch for everybody and there would be roast geese and ducks, their beautiful golden symmetries exposed in large dishes and tantalising gobs of potato-stuffing oozing and bursting from their rear-end stitches. There would be singing and storytelling and laughter and perhaps a tear here and there when absent friends were toasted. There would be gifts for everybody and there would be great good will as neighbours embraced, promising to cherish each other truly till another twelve months had passed.

However, Christmas is an occasion and not a person. A person can do things, change things, create things but all our occasions are only what we want them to be. For this reason Jack's mother waited, Christmas after Christmas, for word of her wandering boy. To other houses would come stout registered envelopes from distant loved ones who remembered. There would be bristling, crumply envelopes from America with noble rectangular cheques and crisp, clean dollars to delight the eye and comfort the soul. There would be parcels and packages of all shapes and sizes so that every house became a warehouse until the great day came when all goods would be distributed.

Now it happened that in our street there was a postman who knew a lot more about its residents than they knew about themselves. When Christmas came he was weighted with bags of letters and parcels. People awaited his arrival the way children awaited a bishop on confirmation day. He was not averse to indulging in a drop of the comforts wherever such comforts were tendered but comforts or no the man was always sensitive to the needs of others. In his heart resided the spirit of Christmas. Whenever he came to the house where the old woman lived he would crawl on all fours past the windows. He just didn't have the heart to go by and be seen by her. He hated to disappoint people, particularly old people. For the whole week before Christmas she would take up her position behind the faded curtains, waiting for the letter which never came.

Finally the postman could bear it no longer. On Christmas Eve he delivered to our house a mixed bunch of cards and letters. Some were from England. He requested one of these envelopes when its contents were removed. He rewrote the name and address and also he wrote a short note which he signed 'your loving son Jack'. Then from his pocket he extracted a ten-shilling note, a considerable sum in those far-off days. He placed the note in the envelope. There was no fear the old woman would notice the handwriting because if Jack was good at some things, as I have already mentioned, he was not good at other things and one of these was writing. In fact, Jack could not write his own name. When the postman came to the old woman's door he knocked loudly. When she appeared he put on his best official voice and said: 'Sign for this if you please Missus.'

The old woman signed and opened the envelope. The tears appeared in her eyes and she cried out loud:

'I declare to God but Jack is a scholar.'

'True for you,' said the postman, 'and I dare say he couldn't get in touch with you until he learned to write.'

'I always knew there was good in him,' she said. 'I always knew it.'

'There's good in everyone Missus,' said the postman as he moved on to the next house.

The street was not slow in getting the message and in the next and last post there were many parcels for the old woman. It was probably the best Christmas the street ever had.

Spreading Joy and Jam

at Christmas

Let him who can boast of no failing take a bow for he is a unique fellow. He is elite among the elite but I would not have his impeccable status for all the lamb on Carrigtwohill.

Carpers will ask why I open on such a vein, what arrant nonsense am I proposing to inflict upon them as winter deepens and Christmas draws near.

I am actually about to recall an outing which took place a week before Christmas, at a time when my hair was black and you'd get a pint for two bob. The hero of the piece is no longer with us but if ever a man was cut out to play Santa Claus, he was that man. He could, in fact, fill any role.

It is many years now since this Mayo friend of mine and I set out for his native county where we proposed to spend a few days carousing and visiting the friends of his boyhood.

As we left Tubbercurry one evening shortly before Christmas on our way into Mayo he recalled the school where he had spent, according to himself, a wasted youth.

His teacher had been a grumpy fellow who regarded my friend and most of the other pupils as irredeemable illiterates and he would warn them day after day that they would never be fit for anything but the most menial of tasks.

'O'Donnell,' he would say to my friend, 'all I want is to see you able to spell for when you go to England your people won't know where you are because you won't be able to write and tell them.'

Actually O'Donnell was able to read and write before ever he went to the national school but he realised that if this fact became known he would find himself out on a limb. His illiterate companions might have no more to do with him. Better, he felt, be a fool among other fools than a star whose brilliance might be his undoing.

When we arrived in Claremorris we stopped at a well-known hostelry. Outside the door we noticed a large van full of jam. There were crates of one-pound and two-pound pots from floor to ceiling.

There was raspberry, strawberry and plum. There was gooseberry, marmalade and mixed fruit.

'It's a terror,' said my friend, 'to see so much

jam exposed to the naked eye and half the world starving.' He shook his head at the injustice of it.

In the bar we treated ourselves to two amber deorums of Irish whiskey and while were sipping from same a young girl entered and approached my friend.

She had somehow mistaken him for the driver of the jam van. In fact he could be mistaken for anybody. He had that kind of face. A woman once gave him a pound to say mass. He had been wearing a dark suit on the occasion.

'Sir,' said the young girl, 'my mother wants to know would you have any cracked pot? Strawberry or marmalade or mixed fruit or anything at all will do.'

'Musha what do you want a cracked pot for?' my friend asked, 'and the van loaded with sound pots.'

'Can I have a pot so sir, a one-pound will do?'

'And has your mother a conveyance?' my friend asked.

'Oh she has sir,' said the girl. 'She has an ass and cart.'

'Tell her to load a few crates,' said my friend, 'but not to overdo it. Ye don't want to make pigs of yeerselves entirely.'

'Oh no sir,' said the girl and she ran from the bar, a transformed creature.

Shortly afterwards we left the pub and proceeded to our car which we had parked nearby. There was no sign of the jam van.

We walked through the town and a delightful walk it was. I would recommend a walk through Claremorris for any and all persons down in the dumps. The friendliness of the people was matched by the cleanliness of the streets and the disposition of the town as a whole.

There were some who came forward and shook our hands, tendering to us the most profuse welcomes to Mayo and the town itself.

One old woman complained of dizzy spells when we enquired after her health. My friend took her pulse and asked if she was taking anything for her complaint. She recalled visits to several doctors and reeled off a long list of medicines. None had done her any good. She seemed to be growing worse rather than better. My friend shook his head as he listened.

'Do you take a lot of spring water?' he asked after he had heard all he wanted to hear.

'Only in tea,' she said, 'and mostly from the tap.'

'Drink plenty spring water,' he advised. 'Spring water never did anybody any harm.'

The old woman nodded eagerly.

'Eat plenty vegetables,' he went on, 'especially cabbage and take a drop of the hot stuff morning and night.'

'I declare to God and His blessed Mother,' said she, 'but I feel better already. It was God sent you this way. I'll pray for you.'

'Pray for us all,' said my friend and he strolled off in the direction of the mountains or more particularly in the direction of Ballyhaunis where he had a large number of relations from his mother's side. I was left holding the baby as it were.

'Is he a doctor?' the old woman asked.

'No,' I informed her, 'he's not a doctor.'

'A specialist then?' she asked hopefully.

'Yes,' I replied, 'he's a specialist.'

Of course he was a specialist, a specialist in cheering people up and a specialist in dispersing gloom.

Eventually we found ourselves driving out of town. A slight mist was drifting down.

In Mayo mists don't fall down. They drift down. We drove slowly. There was no need for words between myself and this natural dispenser of goodness.

'Glory be to God!' he exclaimed when we beheld an ass and cart on the left hand side of the road. At each side of the body sat a female. One was shawled and old. The other was young and beautiful. Their faces were radiant with happiness and contentment.

In the cart were two cases of jam; one was filled with one pound pots and the other with two pound pots. He lowered the window of the car and saluted the pair. The girl waved at him ecstatically. Turning to me he said, 'Were we to depart life now we would surely see heaven for the happiness we spread this day.'

The Voice of an Angel

A drunken Santa Claus is better than no Santa Claus. I heard the remark in the kitchen of a neighbour, a genuinely frustrated mother of seven whose spouse had not returned as promised from an alcoholic excursion downtown where, as he maintained afterwards, he had been waylaid as he was about to return home by some whiskey-sodden companions from his childhood. Sensing that he would not return in time Maggie Cluney, that was the unfortunate mother's name, looked speculatively in my direction but after a brief inspection shook her head ruefully.

In those days I was a lathy, bony youngster about seven stones adrift, especially in the midriff, from an acceptable Santa Claus. The only other person in the kitchen over the age of ten was Maggie's sister Julie Josie who had earlier intimated that she was drunk, which had given rise to the opening statement of our narrative.

After an hour's coaxing and two steaming hot whiskeys we convinced her that nobody would fit the bill as she would. Drowsily, giddily she rose and inarticulately informed us that she was returning to her maidenly abode so that she could sleep off the excess spirits to which she was unaccustomed. Before she managed to stagger through the doorway we ushered the children out into the backyard and burdened her with the Santa Claus outfit from false beard to long boots, from tasselled headgear to vermilion greatcoat and finally the bag of gifts, one for every member of the household.

No great notice would be taken of her in the streets. She lived around the corner and besides there would be many other Santa Clauses abroad in various stages of inebriation but most would be sober and composed, conscious of the sacred missions with which they had been entrusted. Our particular one, Julie Josie, made her way homewards without mishap and also made it upstairs to her single bed where she fell instantly asleep.

Soon the room was filled with gentle snores, even and rhythmical, sonorous and richly feminine, snores that somehow suggested that deep in her subconscious was the need of a male companion who might take the sting out of the frost of life and fulfil her in a manner beyond the capacity of seasonal whiskey. In her sober everyday world she would never admit to any need whatsoever and often when questioned jocosely about her single state she would belittle all members of the opposite sex with a vehemence that made some believe she protested too much. For all that she was a good sister and a good aunt and an even better sister-in-law for she would always present herself *in loco parentis* whenever her sister gave birth and was a great favourite with her nephews, nieces and brother-in-law for the duration of her sister's confinement.

The night wore on until the ninth hour and it was precisely at this time that Julie Josie rose from her unassailable bed. She betook herself to a downstairs room where she donned the Christmas paraphernalia. She slung the bag of gifts across her shoulder and made her way to her sister's house where she was warmly received by her brother-in-law who insisted that she fortify herself with a drop of whiskey before the distribution of the gifts. Then and only then were the children called from the two small, happily overcrowded bedrooms adjoining the kitchen.

The younger ones held back in awe whilst the older ones rushed forward to greet their beloved aunt, pretending as they did that she was really Santa Claus. Some people become imbued with the true spirit of Christmas when they don the red coat and Julie Josie was one of these. After the gifts were distributed they all sat around the fire, the children drinking lemonade and eating Christmas cake, the oldsters sipping whiskey and telling tales of bygone days when geese were really geese and Christmases were always white, when ghosts of loving ancestors whispered in the chimney and a tiny infant was turned away because there was no room at the inn.

Between the whiskey and the sentimental recall many a tear was shed. There were some in the neighbourhood who would say that Julie Josie shed enough tears at Christmas to float the *Titanic*. She was, truly, a sentimental soul, well meaning and generous to a fault. Several whiskeys after her arrival she announced that it was time to go home. She refused all offers of assistance and even more adamantly refused to hand over her Christmas gear. She knew her way home didn't she! Wasn't she going back there now for the thousandth time and anyway what could possibly befall anybody at Christmas when men's hearts were full of goodness even if their bellies were full of beer!

She was, alas, drunker than she thought for she by-passed the corner which led to her house and went downtown in the general direction of the parish church. Mindless of her error she hummed happily to herself staggering to left and right and executing one daring stagger of record proportions which took her first backwards and then forwards, then hither and then thither, until she had travelled the best part of a hundred yards. Had her ever-increasing momentum not been arrested by the parish priest, Canon Coodle, she might well have wound up in the suburbs or even on the bank of the river which circled the town.

Luckily for Julie Josie the canon was a man of considerable girth and without any great strain he steadied the drunken representation of Christmas which wound up in his arms. Although a moderate imbiber himself he always made allowance for those who took a drop in excess on special occasions. He might shake his great, leonine head reproachfully when confronted by extreme cases and he might deliver the occasional sermon condemning the evil of over-indulgence to the detriment of the drunkard's wife and family but he never got carried away. If he had a fault, poor fellow, it was that he suffered from absent-mindedness. This was perhaps why he failed to identify the party who had collided with him. He presumed, and who would blame him, that the creature was male so he did what he always did with unidentified drunks. He directed this one to a warm room over the garage as he had all the others over the years, placed the now incoherent Julie Josie sideways on the bed and left her to her own devices convinced that she was a man and would sleep off the drink in a matter of hours before returning to wife and children.

As he tip-toed down the stairs the reassuring snores convinced him that all would be well in the course of time.

Earlier that night another intoxicated soul was chosen at random to fill the role of Santa Claus although he had never done so before, having neither chick nor child.

His name was Tom Winter and indeed it would have to be said that he looked wintry even in the height of summer for the poor fellow had a perpetually blue nose and was almost always a-shiver.

It was widely held by authoritative sources that he was generally emerging from a skite or booze or bender, call it what you will. Those who knew him best would explain that he only drank at weekends but that he drank so much during those particular days he spent the following five days recovering.

He was the proprietor of a small hardware business specialising in such commodities as sweeping brushes, mousetraps and chamber pots and, of course, nails, screws, hinges and what-have-you. He carried a considerable amount of his stock on his person. His waistcoat pockets, for instance, would be filled with shoelaces and his coat pockets with scissors, penknives and screwdrivers while his trousers' pockets played host to less dangerous articles such as picture cord and pencil toppers. Whatever the customer needed, provided it wasn't a plough or a mowing machine, he would generally find it in a matter of moments on one of his shelves or in one of his pockets.

At six o'clock in the evening he closed his premises and partook of a large cheese sandwich and a double gin before proceeding happily to his favourite tavern where it was his wont to indulge until closing time throughout the weekend and on festive occasions such as Christmas, Easter and St Patrick's Day or, of course, any other special occasion which might provide him with a break from routine.

Tom Winter, for all his wintry features, was a warm-hearted chap, gregarious in his own fashion so long as he didn't have to converse with more than two persons at the same time. He always bought his round and he frequently stood drinks to those who were less well off than himself or seemed that way.

Often it would occur to him that he drank too much and that he was wasting his life. His conscience would prick him from time to time and suggest that he might more profitably pursue some health-giving pursuits but, alas, when a weak-willed man wrestles with his conscience all the weight is on his side and the conscience is the victim of an unfair contest. So it was on Christmas Eve that Tom Winter found himself in the heel of the evening sitting on a high stool with a whiskey-sodden companion at either side of him.

Then a tall, thin, coatless man with his long, grey hair trailing behind his poll and ears dashed into the premises and allowed his gaze to wander from face to face. The obviously demented creature shook his head in despair and then his eyes alighted upon Tom of the wintry dial. He raised an imperial finger which greatly alarmed Tom for he thought at first that the new arrival was either a ghost or a madman. After taking further stock Tom recognised the intruder as a refugee from the northern part of the town, a sober hard-working chap with a large family and an even larger missus who kept him on his toes and who no doubt had dispatched him on some impossible mission on the very eve of Christmas.

Tom's alarm grew even greater when he noticed that the henpecked unfortunate was beckoning him. It was as though he had been summoned by an ancient and pietistic patriarch of superhuman power for he found himself dismounting from his stool. For the first time in his life he began to feel how the twelve apostles felt when they were called from their various vocations to follow the man whose birthday was at hand. The grey-haired elder caught Tom Winter by the sleeve of his coat and led him out of doors. His companions were to say afterwards that Tom's normally wintry features had assumed a radiance that lighted up his head like an electric bulb. They would concede that it had been already moderately lighted by the intake of seven large gins and corresponding tonics but as he left the premises in the wake of the coatless messiah it seemed as though a halo was about to encircle his head and shoulders.

Outside in the night air the coatless one explained his predicament. His brother-in-law, at the best of times an unreliable sort, had promised to fill the role of Santa Claus and was now nowhere to be found. Would Tom, out of the goodness of his heart, do the needful and don the red coat so that the poor man's seven children would continue to keep faith with Christmas!

Tom was about to decline when the coatless wretch fell to his knees and set up such a pitiful wailing that only a man with a heart of stone could continue to hold out. A stream of semi-coherent supplications that would bring tears from a cement block assailed Tom's ears.

'If,' the kneeling figure was wailing, 'I don't come back home with some sort of Santa Claus she'll have my sacred life!'

Tom could only deduce that the grovelling wretch was referring to his outsize wife whose shrill voice could be heard above the wind and the rain during the long nights when fits of dissatisfaction soured her and she became discontented with her lot. She had been known to assault her terrified husband with rolling pins, cups, mugs and saucers and once with an iron kettle which necessitated the insertion of twenty-three stitches.

'Get up and behave like a man.' Tom Winter now adopted a wintry tone which had the effect of putting an end to the wailing. It was obvious that the poor creature was without backbone and if the right tone was adopted would obey any command. He struggled to his feet clutching wildly at Tom lest that worthy attempt to flee. Hope replaced the look of despair in his eyes as he babbled out his gratitude like a puling infant who has been lifted from the cradle.

On their weary way to the anguished fellow's abode Tom had the foresight to enquire if there was any gin on the premises.

'Gin!' came the echo.

'Yes!' Tom raised his voice and made several gin-swallowing motions.

'There may not be gin there now,' came the immediate and generous response, 'but there will be gin,' and so saying the greatly addled victim of wifely abuse dashed back into the pub and returned at once with a bottle of gin. Not only did he bring gin but under his other oxter was a bag containing several bottles of tonic water. Since he could not shake his hand for fear of damage to the bottles Tom Winter slapped him on the back in appreciation of his thoughtfulness.

When they arrived at the abode in question it was decided that they should use the back entrance so that the game might not be given away to the children. There, sure enough, hanging from a cobwebbed rafter was the Santa Claus coat, the Santa Claus hat and the Santa Claus beard. There were no long boots and for this Tom was grateful.

His companion acted as dresser and in jig time Tom was indistinguishable, boots apart, from any other of the numerous Santa Clauses who roamed the country that night. It was agreed that the man of the house should first enter and announce that he had seen Santa Claus in the vicinity and that they should prepare some gin and tonic for his arrival.

A liberal glass of gin was poured and some tonic water added. The lady of the house whose name was Gladiola announced that she had developed a pain in the back as a result of the stress she had endured because of the absence of Santa Claus. She was presented with an equally liberal dollop of gin.

'Hush!' Gladiola raised a silencing hand and then entering fully into the spirit of the business called, 'methinks I hear a step!'

Suddenly everybody from the youngest to the oldest was silent and indeed there was, sure enough, the sound of footsteps in the backyard. Then the back door of the kitchen opened and there entered with his tail in the air the family tomcat who had just returned from an amorous expedition to another part of town. He was followed by Santa Claus. The younger children hid behind their mother while the others crowded round their most welcome visitor and shook his hand and sang and danced and jumped atop the table while their father saw to it that their visitor was presented with his glass of gin into which, without delay, he made substantial inroads.

After the presents were distributed Tom sat by the fire and was prevailed upon to accept another glass of gin.

'I will. I will,' he replied good-humouredly, 'but only if the lady of the house is having one too.'

The lady in question was more than agreeable and soon there was a half-empty bottle where there had been a full one. Songs were sung and for all his wan, woebegone, winterish appearance Tom sang as warmly as any and since he was the proprietor of a soft mellow voice was much in demand as the night wore on.

For once the lady of the house did not resort to abusive language nor did she raise a hand in anger to her husband. Instead she addressed herself to the second gin bottle for which the man of the house had dispatched his oldest daughter. Did I say that he indulged in a glass or two himself? If I didn't let me say at once that he did and if I didn't say that he laughed and sang you may now take my word for it that he did and that he danced as well especially with the smaller members of the household.

The time passed happily and Tom Winter was obliged to admit to himself that he had never spent a better night. No sooner had the second gin bottle been emptied than the clock struck twelve. Declining all offers of tea and edibles Tom took his leave of the happy family in the fond hope that the pub he had vacated earlier in the night would be still manned by some of its staff for much as he enjoyed the household gin he, like all gin lovers, would, if asked, agree that there was no gin like the gin that comes across a bar counter. It is more natural for one thing and there is the unique atmosphere and there is the incomparable presence of drunken companions.

At the doorway, after he had made his goodbyes to the children, Tom Winter gave his word to Gladiola and her husband that he would do the needful without fail the following Christmas and during every Christmas thereafter while there was a gasp of life left in his body. Forgetting to disrobe, he turned his head towards his favourite watering hole. Although full to the gills with gin already he felt an insatiable desire to be reunited with the distinct camaraderie of that spot which had cheered him so often in the past. It is an astonishing aspect entirely of the toper's life that he most requires drink when he least needs it. No other thought now occupied Tom Winter's mind but the prospect of downing a glass of gin and tonic. Let the sot or the drunkard be mightily overburdened after his intake he will, nevertheless, always manage to find room for one more.

After many a skip and many a stagger he eventually arrived at his destination but there was, alas, no room at the inn, at least there was no room for Tom so early on the morning of Christmas Day.

In the eye of the drinker there is no sight so sad as an empty public house or worse a public house which has retained its maximum number of clients and is not prepared, for the sake of comfort and safety, to admit any more. He thought he heard the tinkling of glasses and chinking of coins in tills behind the closed doors, behind the shuttered windows. He had never in his life felt so lonely. It seemed as if the whole world had gone off and left him behind all alone.

Disconsolately he directed his steps towards his shop. Some time later, after it seemed that he had been walking all night, he realised that he had been going around in circles and it dawned on him that the reason for his aimless wandering might be because he really didn't want to go home. To begin with there was nobody there, no cat or no dog, not even a mouse for he had trapped them all in his many mousetraps. Again, more firmly this time, he directed his steps towards the shop but walk as he would he found himself no nearer his base.

Was there a superhuman force restraining him, keeping him away from calamity or was he so drunk that it was not within his power to focus himself properly? There came a time in his journeying when it seemed that he was destined to go on forever and then he fell into the benign arms of Canon Cornelius Coodle. At this stage he had been in the process of passing out.

'My poor fellow,' the canon spoke gently as he dragged his stupefied find towards the garage and thence to the warm room upstairs where he deposited him upon the bed already occupied by the first Santa Claus. Canon Coodle had been surprised to see the first Santa Claus. He had totally forgotten but was relieved that no harm had come to the creature. He was quite taken by the fetching snores, not at all like those to which he was accustomed. He satisfied himself that the second Santa was in no danger of suffocating and was pleased to acknowledge his first resounding snore. He stood for a while at the head of the stairs, listening intently, a rapturous smile on his ancient and serene countenance. He reminded himself that he must tell his curates about this remarkable phenomenon in the morning but wait! What phenomenon! He racked his brains for several moments and then it came back to him. It was the harmonised snoring. Never in all his days had he heard anything so agreeable. It was as though the pair on the bed had been training together all their lives such was the perfect complimentary pitch of their joint renditions. He was reminded of a lyric by Thomas Moore:

Then we'll sing the wild song it once was such pleasure to hear When our voices commingling breathed like one on the ear.

Surely this was a phenomenon or was it more! Was it a minor miracle, an act of homage to the creator on Christmas morning! He hurried downstairs for his tape recorder. Alas when he returned the snoring had ceased altogether and the pair now lay side by side breathing deeply and evenly, their white beards rising and falling as the air expelled itself from their lungs. Again he thought of Thomas Moore but resorted to parody in order to suit the occasion:

Where the storms that we feel in this wide world might cease And our hearts like thy snoring be mingled in peace.

Raising his hand he breathed a blessing upon the contented pair before finally repairing to his bed and to the sleep he so richly deserved. As the night wore on the couple on the bed resorted occasionally to bouts of the melodious snoring heard earlier. Then came the dawn and Julie Josie stirred in her bed but did not open her eyes. Her head, surprisingly, did not throb nor did her heart thump. She lay contented for a while in the belief that she was in her own bed. When the snore erupted from somewhere beside her, some place too close for comfort, she too erupted and would have taken instant flight had she not become aware of her apparel.

She stood astonished looking down at the figure on the bed. She crept close to the recumbent form and gently removed the beard. She could scarcely believe her eyes. She knew Tom Winter well, had shopped with him, had always purchased her hardware wants from Tom and Tom alone and she recalled how at that very moment four different pictures hung from walls in her home, hung by Tom's picture cord from Tom's nails, which he had himself driven, and found to be good nails. She also recalled how her late father had purchased the hammer which had driven the nails.

She knew Tom to be a gentle soul, a good-hearted chap who should not be judged on the strength of his wintry face alone. She decided to wake him. He raised himself slowly to his elbows and was surprised, to say the least, when he beheld Santa Claus standing by the bed.

'I'm sorry I didn't bring you anything,' the voice said and what a voice! It is surely the voice of an angel, Tom told himself. He had never heard an angel's voice but he had imagined such a voice ringing in his ear one day and calling him to heaven if he was lucky, if he was very, very lucky. The voice he had just heard was the kind of voice which had called him in his more hopeful dreams.

'Did we sleep together?' he asked falteringly.

'Looks like it,' she answered with a laugh.

'In that case,' said Tom solemnly, 'you must marry me. In fact,' he continued hardly believing himself to be possessed of such courage, 'I would marry you if we had never slept together. I have admired you many a time on the streets and in my humble shop which you have enhanced by your all too rare visits. Say you'll marry me and make my life into something glorious and good. Marry me and change my ways.'

She took his hand gently and was surprised to see that he was not in the least winterish at close quarters.

'We will talk about it some other time,' she whispered gently.

'I will give up the gin,' he promised, 'and never touch the accursed stuff again.'

'No need to give up all drink though,' came the pragmatic response. 'I firmly believe that a few beers now and then would stand you in better stead.' She looked at her watch and saw that it was twenty-five minutes to eleven.

'I'll have to hurry,' she said, 'if I'm not to miss mass.'

'So must I,' he told her.

'Have you any idea how we arrived here?' she asked. He shook his head. As they divested themselves of their Santa Claus coats she spoke again. 'There is something very strange about all this,' she ventured.

'I know. I know,' Tom agreed. 'It's as though we were destined to be together. I mean why else would God join us together in this most unlikely place without either one of us knowing the first thing about it. Neither of us have any idea how we came to be here.'

They never would because the incident would have slipped Canon Coodle's mind after his breakfast and it would never surface again not even when he would marry them in the summer of the following year. He would baptise their children too in the years that followed and they would both live to see their children grow up and their grandchildren and even their great-grandchildren so that it could be truly said of them that they both lived happily ever after.

A Christmas Diversion

At seventy-one the Badger MacMew retained most of the brown, grey-streaked hair which had earned him his sobriquet. Otherwise he didn't look in the least like a badger. He was tall, slender, elegant and courteous which was more than could be said for some of the mischievous neighbours who privately compared him to the carnivorous mammal after which he was named.

'It isn't fair,' Mary Agge Lehone was fond of telling the few elderly customers who still frequented her tiny green grocery near the end of the long street which had seen better days.

'I mean,' Mary Agge would go on, 'he's so refined and he never badgers anybody. He brings me bags of kindling all the time and he never charges anything. It's all out of the goodness of his heart.'

Part of what Mary Agge said was true. The Badger MacMew, particularly during the long winters, would scour the nearby woodlands for the kindling with which the bright turf fires of the neighbourhood were started.

Though never full, the rickety turf shed at the rear of the Lehone premises was never without a horse-rail or two of turf, not top-quality black turf but sods of brown and grey which burned all too quickly. Black, bottom-sod turf, on the other hand, lasted from one end of the day to the other provided, of course, the fire was properly constructed in the first place.

The Badger's turf shed, several doors downwards from Mary Agge's, contained no turf at all. There was some timber and a modest heap of *bruscar*. Since the Badger lived off his old-age pension he could not afford to supplement his wood stocks with turf or coal. By careful management and skilful disposition of his *bruscar* his hearth was never without a small fire while he was indoors. Electricity was still waiting in the wings in those distant days so that it was to native timber and turf that the street's inhabitants turned to keep out the cold and boil the water and cook the food and wash the clothes and the faces and the hands and the bodies and so forth and so on.

Before we proceed further it must be said that it wasn't altogether out of the goodness of his heart that the Badger MacMew saw to the kindling wants of Mary Agge Lehone. The Badger had, all his life, shown a preference for the single state. Mary Agge's late husband Walter had expired suddenly some thirty years before while cleaning the family chimney. The exertions had proved too much for him and when he fell silently to the ground he was already dead. Mary Agge had been thirty-seven at the time and while she might have married during the intervening years she declined many a substantial offer for she was dainty, petite and some said good-looking in her own way. She also had her own home, fronted by the small green grocery. She knew how to cook and even her detractors would be forced to admit that she never put a hard word on anybody. She received the blessed sacrament every morning of the week and was one of the four select female trios who decorated the altars of the parish church, unfailingly, when it was their turn to do so.

The Badger, on the other hand, missed mass on occasion and received the sacred host but yearly. He was, however, it was agreed by most, not a bad chap at all and might well see heaven if he mended his ways ever so slightly. He suffered occasionally from severe twinges of arthritis but was otherwise healthy and mobile. He had been a trousers-maker until his sixty-eighth year when his arthritic fingers began to fail him and he was forced into retirement.

When Mary Agge's husband Walter died many felt that she would succumb to grief and die of a broken heart but surprisingly she rallied as most widows do and proceeded to live out her lonely days as content as any woman could be in such a situation. The Badger decided shortly after Walter's burial that he would contribute in his own small way to Mary Agge's upkeep. She would never be without kindling while he could visit the woodlands. Gradually he found himself falling in love with her but he resolved that she must never know. For one thing it might damage their friendship such as it was if he ever confessed his true feelings to her. Then there was the danger that she might be so deeply offended that she might sever the relationship permanently. He chose to keep his mouth shut and pray that she might deduce from the quality and consistency of the kindlings that he cherished her above all others and would do so till his last lopping crumbled silently into the ashes of her hearth. He dreamed of her last thing at night and first thing in the morning. He always maintained to himself that it was a small thing which would acquaint her fully of his love for her, some as yet unimagined occasion which would swing things in his favour, some incident or instrument of fate, some insignificant out-of-the-blue factor from which he might find her securely cradled in his arms, her soft hair brushing his ear lobes and her hazel eyes laughing into his.

In his dreams they travelled widely together, sharing the same tastes, revelling in the wild scenery where they would find themselves at the close of day in the presence of incomparable sunsets.

One would never dream from looking at the Badger MacMew that such romantic thoughts dominated his dreaming but such is the reality of life that we should never be surprised by the romantic aspirations of the most unlikely. All humans aspire through fantasy but nominating oneself for the ultimate honours in a close relationship was an undertaking fraught with hazards. That was the reason the Badger had become a perpetual bidder of time like millions of other no-hopers in every corner of the human world. He was well aware that others in the vicinity were desirous of advancing their causes through fair means or foul in the direction of his beloved Mary Agge. His worst fear was that she might suddenly be swept off her feet by a dark horse in a late surge while he dawdled and hoped for a miracle. In this respect there was one individual he feared more than any other. In his estimation the person in question was a loud-mouthed, scurrilous pervert by the name of Danny Sagru. Every street, he thought bitterly, had its Danny Sagru. He was, therefore, astonished one day to hear the very same scoundrel being described by none other than Mary Agge herself as not a bad oul' fella.

Not a bad oul' fella! He repeated the undeserved delineation to himself several times. Oh dear, oh dear! How naive was womanhood and how gormless was this unfortunate woman in particular!

Danny Sagru was, without doubt, the most unpopular man in the entire street, the entire parish. If you were to scour the highways and byways you would be hard put to find somebody with a good word to say about him. There were a number of reasons for this. He owned most of the land roundabout. He was wealthier than even Tom Shine the draper, Joe Willies the baker, Ned Hobbs the grocer.

Danny Sagru didn't carry his wealth well. He boasted about it. He rattled the silver in his trousers pockets and he regularly flicked the chunky wad of notes which he had no need to carry about with him.

If he ever gave a small boy a penny he would always charge the recipient to inform all and sundry that Danny Sagru had given it to him.

He never subscribed to charities and yet Mary Agge Lehone had publicly stated that he was not a bad oul' fella. He was an oul' fella all right, the Badger would subscribe to this. He was several years older than the Badger although he did not look as if he was. He had an appetite like a horse but wait, the Badger began a reassessment of his arch-rival.

If he was placed under oath the Badger would have to admit that the scoundrel possessed a certain degree of spurious loyalty. He would have to concede that Danny Sagru always purchased his vegetables from Mary Agge Lehone and from Mary Agge Lehone alone. Let the cabbage be wrinkled, the spuds watery, the turnips frostbitten. Let her parsnips be shrivelled, her carrots shrunken, her cauliflowers browning! It mattered not to Danny and there was another even more worrying aspect of his purchases. He never questioned her prices. There was an extravagance about him as he pressed the coins into the cup of her hand.

'Your change, your change,' she would call after him as he exploded through the shop door, cabbages in one hand, potato satchel in the other.

'Keep it, keep it,' he would call back as though it were a considerable sum, whereas in reality, it never exceeded a half-penny.

For all his wealth Danny Sagru had never forsaken the modest home where he first saw the light. The house, like all the others including Mary Agge's, was two-storeyed and two-bedroomed with a back shed, always filled to capacity with black, heavy sods. There was access from the shed to a long but narrow backway along which ran the seventy or more back sheds which housed the fuel supplies for the corresponding front or street houses. All looked alike, all with pitch painted corrugated iron roofs, all rickety and in need of restructuring, all save that of Danny, which was a model of its kind and which was crammed from bottom to top with turf sods as black as the ace of spades, heavy as lead and more lasting than coal.

Danny had several suppliers who were acquainted from long experience with his precise needs. Turf-cutters with horse-drawn, clamped rails of the precious bottom sods would arrive regularly at the Sagru shed and deposit their loads. There was a fixed rate and seasoned turf-cutters would say to novices, 'You don't renege on him and he won't renege on you. You'll get nothing extra but you will get your due.'

Then, as happens every ten years or so, there came a poor turf harvest. The less well-off suffered most. Danny Sagru suffered not at all. Widows and waifs in the vicinity might perish with the cold but Danny held fast to the sods he had. His poorer neighbours knew that it would be a waste of time to plead for a sod or two to tide them over till the bogs dried so that suppliers might gain access to their turf banks. Like the Badger MacMew they traversed the woodlands near and far for kindling.

The Badger led parties of youngsters to likely places where old logs had lain rotting for years. They sawed and hacked and somehow managed to acquire hearthfuls of fuel to see them through. All the while, through the long nights, Danny Sagru sat in front of his warm fire, occasionally adding to the brightness and redness of his ulcerous nose by the simple expedient of swallowing glass after glass of punch. None shared his hearth, no dog nor cat nor chick nor child nor neighbour nor friend. What he savoured he savoured alone.

Alas for Mary Agge Lehone her fires grew smaller but they never went out. The Badger MacMew saw to that. The Badger gave all he had until the frost silently laid its cold, white mantle over field and bogland, over street, backway and rooftop. The frost was but a day in residence when Danny Sagru was astonished by the inroads the bad weather had made into his turf. Instead of tackling his spirited pony to the gleaming trap as was his wont when he wished to visit an outlying cattle fair he hired a hackney car to transport him across the fifteen miles of roadway to the village where the fair would be in progress. With Christmas coming up in a few days and fodder in short supply there would be little demand for store cattle. It was a good time to buy and a man with fodder to spare and money to burn like Danny Sagru might profitably expand his existing stock at no great expense. He had done so many times in the past and, indeed, it was from such fortuitous investments that he built most of his fortune. As they drove towards the village Danny's attention was drawn to a moving vehicle which slowly descended a hilly boreen on its way to the main road.

'Pull up! Pull up!' Danny called to his driver. As the road-bound transport reached the cross which would take it to the village where the fair was in progress Danny emerged from the rear of the hired car and raised a hand, indicating that he had a desire to parley. Before him was stalled at the crossroads one of the largest, highest-clamped, heaviest loads of black turf ever to present itself before the greedy green eyes of Danny Sagru. The load was drawn by a powerful black mare, sixteen hands high and shimmering with muscle from crest to hock, a beautiful animal and worthy transporter of such a perfectly clamped cargo.

'How much?' Danny Sagru asked.

The turf-man, squat and brown, looked over his merchandise as if he had only then noticed it and took stock of the prosperous-looking individual who posed the question regarding the price.

'One pound, two shillings and sixpence,' came the clipped response.

Danny advanced and circled the mare and rail, feeling individual sods as he proceeded with his inspection.

'If you'll be good enough to move out of the way now, like a good chap,' the turf-man flicked his reins, 'I'll be on my way, for you see sir I have clients galore waiting in the village.'

'Hold it! Hold it!' Danny Sagru raised an imperious hand and blocked his way. The mare shook her shining harness and raised her shapely head with its sensitive nose and flickering ears.

'I'll give you your money,' Danny announced calmly, 'but you'll have to deliver to my premises in Ballyfurane.'

'Which is seven miles from here and seven miles back and which adds another shilling to the price, for this mare will be in sore need of oats by the time we deliver.' The turf-man folded his arms.

'I won't quibble with you.' Danny located the money and handed it over.

'You'll give me a luck penny now!' Danny suggested to the turf-man who was quick to point out that luck money only came into question when large sums were involved.

'Do you know me?' Danny asked.

'Sure don't the whole world know you,' the turf-man declared.

'Ask any person you meet on your way into town

and they'll show you where I hang out,' Danny informed him. 'The turf shed is at the rear of the house and 'tisn't bolted nor locked for as quirky and quare as my neighbours are they're too proud to steal. Off with you now and who knows but we'll do business again.'

'Ballyfurane is out of my way,' the turf-man announced as he allowed the mare her head, 'but if the money is right I could see myself doing further business with you.'

The village of Ballyfurane consisted of one long main street and two small side streets. The windows of the small shops along the main thoroughfare were decorated with holly and ivy. Some boasted tinsel and fairy lights and a few sported homemade cribs representing the nativity.

With Christmas approaching there was an air of mild anticipation. Shoppers were plentiful and business, if not brisk, was reasonably good, which was just about as good as anybody could expect in a small place like Ballyfurane.

When the Angelus bell tolled in memory of the Incarnation, as it did every day at twelve noon, Badger MacMew found himself standing at the quietest of the village's four street corners. His hands were thrust deep into his trousers pockets and there was a faraway look on his unshaven face. He was, however, far from despondent. He had, but a bare five minutes before, delivered a bundle of high-quality kindling to Mary Agge Lehone and she had actually allowed her fingers to rest briefly on the back of his hand by way of appreciation. With recollection he concluded that it would be fairer to say her fingers brushed the back of his hand. Still it was a handsome advance on the smiles with which she had previously rewarded him.

As he looked into the distance he beheld for the first time the high-clamped rail of turf drawn by the black mare, guided by a turf-man he had never seen before. He withdrew his hands slowly from his pockets and proceeded in a rambling fashion towards the oncoming transport. The Badger was possessed of the natural curiosity of all villagers everywhere except that in his personal case he was a curious fellow by nature and liked to know at all times what was happening in his bailiwick. As he drew near he was surprised when the mare drew to a halt at the behest of the turf-man.

'Excuse me sir!' the turf-man respectfully

addressed himself to the Badger. 'I am looking for the premises of Danny Sagru.'

The Badger did not answer at once. The proprietor of the sought after premises was safely out of town and would not be back for some time, probably nightfall since he was partial to strong drink whenever he encountered fellow-members of the cattle-jobbing confraternity.

'Follow me.' The Badger turned on his heels and led the way to the by-way at the rear of the main street. He kept a distance of forty yards between himself and the turf-man and he walked along the pavements rather than the roadway so that it might be clearly seen that the turfman and he had no connection with each other. Firstly he led the turf-man to a lane-way at the back of which was a by-way which would take them albeit circuitously to the backway behind the main street where the many lookalike turf sheds stood side by side. The backway was deserted save for a neighbourhood tomcat who sat on the roof of a shed and took no interest in the proceedings beneath him. In the backway the Badger slowed his gait so that the turf-man might catch up with him.

'This is the shed.' He indicated the rickety

structure at the rear of Mary Agge Lehone's small shop. 'I'll open the door for you and you can heel it in.'

In no time at all, the rail was empty and the turf-man on his way homewards by an altogether different egress, indicated by the Badger. It was an egress which would lead him to a little-used boreen which would lead him past the village and on to the main route to his hilly abode. Later that evening he and his wife and family would invest the turf money in their Christmas shopping and a happy and holy Christmas would be had by all.

As soon as the turf-man had departed the Badger took it upon himself to call upon Mary Agge. A beaming smile was the essence of her greeting as soon as he entered. They stood there without exchange of words or the need for exchange of words.

'You will find,' the Badger said after a short while, 'a little Christmas gift in your shed and I hope it brings you the warmth and comfort you so richly deserve.'

With that he departed and did not appear on the street again until Christmas Eve. It was nightfall as he walked past her door and at first he thought that the sounds he heard as he went by were the chortlings of a dove but no, it was Mary Agge calling his name, gently ever so gently and but barely discernible even though the street was still. When he entered she closed the door behind them and led the way to the small kitchen where a glowing fire spread heat from the hearth.

'You'll have a drop of whiskey,' she said with a smile, 'and so will I,' and so they did and she invited him back the following day for his Christmas dinner and there was no word from Danny Sagru about his missing turf for he was vain in the extreme and would never give it to say that he had been taken down. It would never occur to him, in a score of years, that the Badger had diverted the turf and that Mary Agge Lehone had burned it.

Indeed the Badger and Mary Agge shared all their Christmas dinners thereafter but not as friends or lovers or anything like that but as man and wife and there need be no worries about their living happily ever after because that was exactly what they did.

Pail But Not Wan

One of my fondest memories of Christmas is a whistling milkman now passed on to that sweet clime where whistle the gentle winds of heaven. He would whistle louder, longer and sweeter at Christmas than at any other time of the year.

He must have been sixty when I first heard him of a Christmas morning many years ago. He was a curly-haired, chubby-faced fellow who looked only thirty years old, although in reality he was double that age. He was that kind of person. Age, it would seem, made no impression on him.

Without doubt his fountain of youth was his whistling. First thing in the morning after the cocks had crowed and the last of the crows flown countrywards his exhilarating serenading could be heard clearly for long distances as he cycled upon his rounds.

What a happy man he must have been! He never whistled a drab melody. He excelled most of all at the stirring march and he would generously empty his heart to all and sundry at no charge whatsoever. Romantic airs were meat and drink to him and he would give his all in an effort to strum the sweet chords of love which lie dormant in so many people.

Dour veterans of the marital confrontation would relent and turn in their beds to celebrate sweet sessions of amorous rapture and all because of his incidental input. No nightingale ever sang so sweetly as he. No skylark ever plumbed the soulful depths for sensitive melody. The early morning, ushered in by the waning stars, was merely the backdrop for his princely renditions.

He contributed more to the rescue of foundering marriages than any human intermediary could ever hope to. It often seemed that he was especially transported from some heavenly sphere for no other purpose than the upraising of downcast hearts. Even his lightweight warblings would fritter away depressions and lift up the human spirit to its loftiest pinnacles.

Surely the pipings of that yesterday milkman had their origins in heaven although it was the orifice of his contracting lips that modulated and measured the bewitching torrent of empyrean sonority which charmed and delighted all those who happened to be within earshot. There wasn't a child in the street who did not try to emulate that dear, departed milkman.

I remember once of an icy morning before Christmas he fell from his rickety bicycle, spilling the contents of both his pails and breaking two front teeth into the bargain. His lips, poor fellow, were brutally lacerated. The tears formed in his eyes as he witnessed the streams of freshly drawn milk coursing irredeemably to the nearest channel but how quickly did he transform misfortune into triumph.

Supporting himself on his right knee and placing his left hand over his breast he pursed his shattered lips, oblivious to the agonising pain. Then extending his right hand to his unseen public he gave the performance of his life. Long before had he finished, the under-employed lips of couples in that once dreary street were never so utilised in the pursuit of loving fulfilment. For the listening lovers in the silent houses it was a never-to-be-forgotten experience. Some had never even dreamed of aspiring to such unprecedented ecstasies. Many had waited a score of Christmases for such a development.

If only the world and its people could wait long enough everybody would eventually be kissed by someone, be loved by someone.

This piece is just an informal salute to Christmas and to the memory of a forgotten milkman who made life more harmonious on a far-off Christmas morning for those within his round.

The Good Corner Boy

This is the story of the good corner boy. As stories go it is as true as any. To some it may seem improbable but I can counter this by stating that most true stories seem that way anyway. Enough, however, of the preamble. Let us proceed without further ado.

On 20 December 1971, Madgie Crane withdrew some of her savings from the bank. A tidy sum was involved: two hundred pounds no less, but then as she might say herself she had many calls. There were sons and daughters and grandchildren. There were neighbours and there were friends and relations. Of husbands she had none. There had been one but he had passed on some years before and she had come to terms with her grief in the course of time.

As she turned the corner which would take her to the post office she bumped accidentally into another woman who chanced to be returning from the same venue. As a result Madgie Crane's purse jumped from the grocery bag where it had been securely wedged between a cabbage and a half-pound of rashers. It landed at the feet of the corner boy in residence and that worthy immediately fenced it between his waiting boots where no trace of it remained visible to the searching eye.

The minutes passed but no move did our corner boy make. He looked hither and thither from time to time but if there had never been a purse between his feet he would have looked hither and thither anyway and he would have looked up and down anyway but he would never have bent to tie his shoes for in all the years that I have spent studying corner boys I never saw one bend to tie his shoes.

As he pretended to look after his laces his delicate fingers quickly opened the purse and his drowsy eyes looked inside. Two hundred pounds if there was a penny! Deftly he flicked the purse up the loose sleeve of his faded raincoat and rose to his feet. Even if somebody had been watching, and he was sure that nobody had, his actions could not possibly convey anything of a disingenuous nature.

It was no more than a formality to insert his hands into his trousers' pockets with the purse still up his sleeve. A gentle shake of the sleeve in question and the purse fell downwards into the waiting pocket. It was precisely at that moment that he was addressed by Madgie Crane. There was a tear in her eye and a quiver in her voice.

'I suppose,' she opened tremulously, 'you saw no sign of a purse.'

No answer came from the seemingly mystified corner boy. It was as though she had spoken in a strange tongue.

'Every penny I had was inside in it,' she continued.

Still no response from the resident corner boy. He blew his nose and he looked hither and thither. He shifted his weight from one foot to the other and he looked secondly at Madgie Crane. He noted the weariness and the confusion and he watched without change of expression as the tears became more copious. Her brimming eyes discharged them aplenty down the sides of her withered face. His hand tightened on the swollen purse and he inclined his head towards the channel which ran parallel to the pavement.

Hard as he would try afterwards he would never be able to explain why he did what he did because he needed money at that point in his life as he had never needed money before. He needed it for his widowed sister with whom he lodged and he needed it for her children whom he loved and he needed it to pay his bills. He needed it so that he might embark on a comprehensive drunk for a day or two for he believed that this was his entitlement because of the season that was in it.

Having inclined his head towards a particular spot in the channel he moved swiftly in that direction and pretended to retrieve the purse. Lifting it aloft he enquired of Madgie Crane if this indeed was the missing article. Madgie chortled with delight and clapped her dumpling hands together soundlessly. She stood on her toes for the first time in twenty years and graciously accepted her property from the hands of her benefactor.

She opened the purse and she proceeded to count her money. Never was there such an assiduous reckoning and never did anyone count so little for so long. Assuring herself that every note was present and correct she instituted a second count and finally, when that was satisfactorily concluded, she started a third count. It was during the middle of this count that she moved off in the direction of the post office where she had deposited her grocery bag with an obliging clerk.

The corner boy stood amazed. He had been stunned and shocked many times in his life but he had never been amazed. It was a strange and unnerving experience for a man of his years. A giddiness assailed him and he collapsed in an ungainly heap at the corner where he had stood rocklike for so long.

A half hour later he woke up in a nearby public house just as an ambulance arrived on the scene. He refused all forms of aid and was told that a doctor was on the way. He declined the publican's offer to wait in the snug but he did not decline the medicinal brandy tendered to him by the publican's wife. Exactly forty-five minutes after his collapse he returned to his corner and took up his usual position.

Word of his good deed spread and the community was shocked to learn that he had received nothing by way of reward from Madgie. No wonder he fainted, some said, and he was right to faint, more said. An ad hoc committee was formed and a collection made. It amounted to eleven pounds two shillings and seven pence half-penny. He wrapped it in his handkerchief and instructed a neighbour who chanced to be passing to deliver it to his sister. For the rest of the day, because it was Christmas time, he answered all queries from passers-by, directing strangers to the post office, the banks and the churches, often accompanying them to the extremes of his bailiwick and imparting his blessing on all. Also because it was Christmas he led the old and the feeble across the busy roadway, cautioning them to alert him whenever they wished to cross back again. Only at Christmas do corner boys involve themselves in the activities around them.

Then a second giddiness assailed him but this time it was accompanied by a sharp pain in the chest. He fell to the pavement where he immediately expired. When word of his passing spread, all who knew him agreed he had been a good corner boy. He never scolded children and he was the last refuge of wandering tomcats who took shelter behind him at night when cross canines might tear them asunder. He was devoted to his corner. Those who knew him would testify that he lived for nothing else and that it was because of his corner he never married.

When drunkards fought or scuffled on their way homewards he never interfered, thereby assuring the impoverished and the curious of free entertainment, unlike others who spoiled the fun by coming between the contestants. His corner would never be the same again nor would we look upon his likes again. Truly it could be said that he died at his post and surely it would be right and fitting to call him the good corner boy.

Something Drastic

Canon Cornelius Coodle stood with his palms on the parapet of Ballybradawn bridge and surveyed the swirling, foaming flood waters below. The canon could never cross any bridge at home or abroad without pausing to inspect the waters that passed beneath. He had once been a salmon angler and was locally regarded as something of an authority on lures, particularly artificial flies and minnows which he frequently made himself. He was of the belief that every major river needed its own particular bait.

Generally speaking, suitable baits were to be found in shops which catered for the needs of anglers but because of the contours of local river beds and because of the related agitation of the changing waters the canon believed that one had to be specific. There were other factors too such as the light and shade peculiar to certain stretches of water influenced by the arboreal canopies at particular times of year. All of these and many other features, too numerous to mention, had to be taken into account when a man sat down to prepare his angling gear for the beginning of the angling season which was no more than ten days away.

Canon Coodle had not fished for several years. Now in his early eighties he lacked the sprightliness which once saw him vault the most formidable of stiles in his stride and leap unerringly from rock to crag to grassy inch where a false step might easily mean permanent immersion or at the very least a broken limb.

As he looked down the river's course he recalled doughty salmon which he had landed in his heyday. A happy smile crossed his face but was at once replaced by a frown for which he could find no apparent justification. This was the worrying part. His memory had started to fail him as well as his physical agility and he wondered what it might be that had occasioned the frown. In vain he tried to bring it to mind. He knew for certain that there was a problem and undoubtedly it was an unpleasant task and it would hang over him until it presented itself at the most unlikely and unfavourable time such as when he might be sitting in his study after dinner smoking his pipe or savouring a sip from the glass of port in which he sometimes indulged after a satisfactory meal. Then the forgotten obligation or predicament would intrude not because he would remember it of his own accord but because it would be thrust upon him by a reminder from his housekeeper or curates or by a visit from the person or persons involved.

Always when making a promise that he would perform a particular function he would start right away in the direction of his study to make a note of the business but by the time he reached pencil and paper he would have forgotten. He was a prudent enough man about the maintenance of his health so that when he found the chill of the river winds penetrating his overcoat he began his return journey to the presbytery.

Every evening before dinner he would walk briskly as far as the bridge and back again. He never dawdled on such excursions. The pangs of hunger and the prospect of an excellent dinner saw to that. It was the only business, apart from celebration of his masses, of which his housekeeper did not need to remind him. It was said of him that he had a good stroke which simply meant in the everyday idiom of the place that he was possessed of a healthy appetite.

Upon his return he knelt for a while in prayer. Then came the persistent tinkling of the housekeeper's bell. After a decent interval he joined his curates in the dining-room. Throughout the excellent meal the talk centred on Christmas duties. It was during dessert that the younger of the curates reminded the canon that he was expected at the local convent at two o'clock on Christmas Day where, as had been the custom for the eighteen years of his canonship, he would be expected to join the sisters for the Christmas dinner.

The curate had been waylaid by Mother Francesca, a towering figure of commensurate girth for whom both curates and their beloved pastor had a healthy respect if not regard.

'Was she born a reverend mother,' a wisecracking bishop had once asked, 'because,' he continued, 'I just cannot imagine her as a novice.'

It would be true to say, however, that Francesca was not as bad as she was painted. All she ever wanted was her own way and as long as that was forthcoming life could be tolerable enough for those who came into contact with her on a regular basis. So that was it then, the canon, relieved after a fashion, pushed away his half-finished dessert and declined the offer of coffee from the senior curate. At the mention of Francesca's name and the awful prospect of the Christmas dinner which he could not avoid he had instantly decided that instead of the glass of port to which he would normally address himself he would finish off the bottle which contained, in his humble estimation, at least three glasses. He felt it was his inalienable right in view of what he would have to suffer shortly as a consequence of parochial custom.

After the port he would go straight to bed for, as he well knew, he would be in no condition to go anywhere else. His curates no longer allowed him to go on sick calls after dark unless it was a special occasion and then only if one of the curates was available to transport him.

The younger men had noted his reaction when reminded of his unwelcome seasonal responsibility. They had both dined with Mother Francesca and they had both been obliged to resort to Vesuvian belches in order to get rid of the trapped winds and obnoxious gases which had built up to dangerous levels after the meals which Francesca insisted on preparing herself, especially if those invited to dine were members of the clergy. She had been brought up to believe that the clergy needed and were entitled to richer, meatier and generally more substantial meals than lay people no matter how pious. The official convent cook, Sister Carmelita, never interfered when her superior became involved. She had been tempted often enough especially during the preparation for the Christmas dinner but like all the other inmates she opted for the peaceful way out and kept her mind to herself.

Christmas, which was not the norm for Christmas days in that part of the world, broke mild and balmy and belied the time of year that was in it. The presbytery housekeeper had taken off at first light on her bicycle for her sister's home in the nearby hills and, after the masses, the curates would head for the homes of their families in the north and south of the diocese.

The canon would look after the sick calls, if any, and one of the curates would return before darkness to relieve the canon who would be in no fit mental condition to go anywhere, anyway, after his ordeal at the convent and it was to this venerable institution that he wended his way shortly before two o'clock on the appointed day to partake of the Christmas fare so lovingly prepared by Mother Francesca.

During Francesca's brief absences from the kitchen Sister Carmelita would furtively and speedily modify the more distasteful aspects of the reverend mother's preparations. 'Otherwise she might poison us all!' she told herself, not without justification.

As Canon Coodle drew near the tree-lined entrance his steps faltered and he cast about him that sort of despairing look which was to be seen on the faces of condemned souls as they ascend the steps to the gallows. Although he tried to banish them, visions of the previous years' dinners began to take shape before his mind's eye. How could he ever forget the monumental heap which covered the huge dish so that not a solitary speck of the esteemed willow pattern was to be seen anywhere beneath. There was, to begin with, a mound of mashed turnips which would comfortably cope with the needs of a small hotel for the round of a day and there was a mighty heap of potato stuffing which would go a long way towards assuaging the hunger pangs of the average family with a grandparent or two thrown in for good measure.

There had been peas and beans, white meat and dark as well as the outsized thigh of the largest cock turkey that could be found in the countryside for miles around and all of this on the same plate, covered with fat-infused gravy. Worst of all, the victims were expected to consume every trace of food on their plates. The canon shuddered at the memory. Mother Francesca always took it as a personal affront if anybody failed to clear the plate. She eschewed containers for the different vegetables, stoutly maintaining that there was too much trouble involved and that, anyway, it was nothing more than grandiose nonsense.

All her charges from young postulants to elderly sisters who had all but forgotten where they originally came from had the foresight to cut down on food intake for days before and especially on Christmas morning with such a challenge looming in front of them. The canon had expressly foregone breakfast so that he would be capable of making inroads into Francesca's plate not to mention her specially enriched plum pudding which followed hot on the heels of the monstrous main course. The plum pudding in turn was followed by Christmas cake and several freshly opened tins of assorted biscuits which had to be liberally sampled and seen to be liberally sampled.

The saddest aspect of the entire orgy as far as Canon Cornelius Coodle was concerned was that not a single drop of intoxicating drink was on display although it would have to be said that this was not entirely the fault of the reverend mother. Rather was it the fault of the canon's predecessor Canon Montague and the reverend mother's predecessor, Mother Amabilis.

The late Canon Montague, poor fellow, had the reputation of being the heaviest drinker in the diocese and would drink any other two clerics under the table, at any given sitting, without exerting himself. His friend Mother Amabilis was what locals would call an innocent sort, that is to say she was a trifle naive as far as the ways of the world were concerned. She would ply the late canon with his favourite poison, Hooter's Heart-throb whiskey, until, I turn to the locals again, it came out through his eyes.

Always, by the time the dinner ended he was incapable of negotiating the journey from convent to presbytery of his own accord. Before he expired at the astonishing age of eighty-nine from sheer senility and a perfectly functioning liver, he had consumed a veritable reservoir of Hooter's Heart-throb. On the Christmas of his eighty-sixth year he was so plied with his favourite tincture by

Mother Amabilis that he was unable to perform his priestly duties for three whole days. Word inevitably reached the bishop of the diocese and, as a consequence, the mother-general paid a surprise visit to Mother Amabilis shortly after Christmas or to be exact on the afternoon of the feast of the Epiphany. She called her aside, as it were, and from that moment forth an embargo was placed on intoxicating drink within the confines of the convent. All existing stocks were transferred to the local hospital where they might be used in moderation for purely medicinal purposes.

Oddly enough Canon Coodle placed not a particle of blame on his otherwise illustrious predecessor or on the open-handed Mother Amabilis. There is none of us who does not suffer in some small way from the sins of our ancestors but the balance is nearly always redressed by the goodness they leave behind.

Canon Coodle, with apologies to none, fortified himself, to a limited degree, by imbibing two glasses of twelve-year-old whiskey prior to his departure for the convent and he now found himself flushed of face but sound in mind and limb, with no prospect of further drink, at the hall door of the convent. He was warmly received and it must be said that there wasn't a nun there, Mother Francesca apart, who would not have gladly lifted the cruel restriction given the authority to do so. There was no doubt but that Mother Francesca had the power to do so because the present incumbent of the bishopric would have yielded to any demand she might make rather than incur her ire.

Francesca, alas, had been born of drunken parents and since there are some who believe that it is better to be born in hell there was no way she would countenance the lifting of the ban on alcohol. Rather than possessing a genuine vocation for her calling the reverend mother was a refugee from the real world and like all refugees she was so thankful to be in a safe haven that she would rather die than invalidate an established procedure.

As the nuns tripped merrily into the spacious dining-room the canon trudged behind escorted by Mother Francesca. They sat according to rank and age along both sides of the table with the canon at the head and the reverend mother at the bottom.

All present then reverentially entwined their fingers and sat rigidly as they waited for the canon to start the proceedings with the Grace Before Meals.

He had but barely concluded when the phone rang. All sat silently in the hope that it would go away but go it did not. Mother Francesca lifted her mighty frame slowly from her seat. What a rugby forward she would have made, the canon almost laughed aloud, if she had been born of the opposite sex, although as she bore down upon the offending phone she looked more like a battleship. A heated argument ensued. It was obvious that the person at the other end of the line was determined to have her way.

'Can't it wait a half hour?' the Reverend Mother shouted. Her frown suggested that the answer was in the negative.

'But he's just about to begin his Christmas dinner, poor man,' the Reverend Mother persisted vehemently. The anger on her face as she listened intimated that the caller did not really care what the canon was sitting down to.

'All right, all right!' the Reverend Mother called at the top of her voice. 'We'll let him decide for himself.'

Meanwhile Canon Cornelius Coodle, vicar general of the diocese and the eldest of its priests, had been an eager listener. Was the possibility of a reprieve on the cards?

'You are required for a sick call,' Mother Francesca spoke as if the canon was to blame, 'but I have suggested to this person,' she distastefully indicated the mouthpiece in her hand, 'that you be allowed finish your dinner first.'

The canon rose to his feet, touching the sides of his mouth with the large white napkin provided by his hosts in an effort to conceal his absolute delight.

'Find out where it is,' he asked gently, 'we must never keep a poor soul waiting.' He laid the napkin on the table and blessed himself although he had neither sipped nor eaten.

'You won't believe this,' the Reverend Mother turned her attention to the nuns who had been highly entertained by the exchanges, 'but they want him to go to the very top of Ballybuggawn at his age without a bite inside in him.' All the nuns tut-tutted obediently and reproachfully.

'I'll have to fetch my car.' The canon was already moving towards the door of the dining-room, his face alight with joy, a surging youthfulness in his step.

'Wait, wait!' Mother Francesca called after him. 'The sisters will drive you as far as your car and you can take your dinner with you.' Here she summoned the younger members of her community and in no time at all a pair of eager sisters appeared from the kitchen with a large wickerwork basket containing the delights already mentioned.

'No need, no need.' The canon raised his hands aloft. It required his best efforts to control his happiness. He wanted to leap, to shout, to dance while Mother Francesca lifted the white cloth which covered the massive array of goodies which they had prepared for him. He feigned inexpressible gratitude and announced that he would do justice to the fare before the night was out. Then he was gone, followed by the two nuns who bore the basket between them. They would deposit it in the boot of his car on his instructions and he would proceed airily to Flanagan's of Ballybuggawn and, if it was on top of the highest hill in the parish itself, he wouldn't have minded were it twice as high or the road twice as dangerous. He was a free man and, more importantly, a clergyman on his way to succour some unfortunate soul who desperately needed forgiveness. Otherwise why would he or she seek the services of a priest on Christmas Day?

Canon Coodle regretted that he would not be able to keep his promise about doing justice to the contents of the basket but he promised himself that it would not be thrown away untouched. With this in mind he drew to a halt near an iron gate which led to a green field half-way up the hill of Ballybuggawn. A large flock of crows had just alighted thereon and who better to consume and relish an unwanted meal than the birds of the air. Entering the field, basket in hand, he looked all around to see if anybody was watching. He need not have worried. Man, woman and child in the area were sitting down to dinner or had finished dinner and were resting.

Then, hastily, he unceremoniously dumped the entire convent dinner and returned each plate to the basket before going back to his car. Nobody would ever know and when Mother Francesca would ask if he had enjoyed his Christmas dinner he could truthfully reply that it had gone down well and there wasn't a single one of the crows, already gorging themselves with delighted squawks, who would contradict him. He stood contentedly, hands clasped behind back, surveying the snow-covered summit of Ballybuggawn. He brought his hands to his midriff and entwined them prayerfully as he expressed his gratitude to the Lord of Creation for his happy lot. If, at the end of his days, he should be asked to nominate the happiest day of his life he would have no hesitation in selecting the day that was in it.

At Flanagan's of Ballybuggawn he was well received. Here in this humble cot he was respected above all other men in the parish for his humility and saintliness. Joe and Sarah Flanagan, a childless couple in their late seventies, were mystified when the canon asked to be shown into the presence of the sick party. As the elderly pair continued to exchange baffled looks the canon announced that he would administer the sacrament of Extreme Unction without further delay.

'I'm afraid there's been a mistake Canon,' Joe Flanagan forestalled him, 'there's nobody sick here.'

Joe's wife Sarah curtsied and spoke next. 'We haven't been sick a day thank God these fifty years Canon,' she said proudly.

'And is there another Flanagan in the neighbourhood?' the canon asked politely.

He was informed with equal politeness that he was looking at the only two Flanagans on Ballybuggawn Hill from top to bottom.

'And is there anybody in need of a priest hereabouts?' the canon ventured. No. There was nobody sick in the vicinity thank God but might it not be some other Flanagan in some other part of the parish?

'Oh dear, oh dear!' Canon Coodle looked out through the small window of the kitchen and saw that the first stars were beginning to appear prematurely as dusk embraced the snow-crested hill.

'It's a long journey back to town Canon,' Joe Flanagan reminded his parish priest.

'And a cold one Canon,' Sarah Flanagan was curtsying again.

'Would you take a drop of something Canon,' Joe Flanagan asked in a most respectful tone, 'a tint of the hot stuff now for the journey?'

'Or there's port,' Sarah put in. 'Sandeman's Five Star, or there's brandy if you'd care for it?'

'Port,' the canon divested himself of his overcoat and took the chair which Joe had moved closer to the fire; 'a port would be much appreciated.'

An hour later after the canon had swallowed a large glass of port and eaten two boiled eggs with several slices of homemade brown bread the trio knelt and recited the Rosary after which the canon thanked his hosts from the bottom of his heart and assured them that he had never eaten such flavoursome eggs or such nourishing bread in his entire life.

The trio had concluded earlier that the canon had been the victim of a mischievous joke and privately the canon could not find it in his heart to condemn the mischief-maker if such indeed it was. Reluctantly he took his leave and promised faithfully that he would visit for his supper again when the snow had departed from the hilltop and the slopes brightened by the lengthening days.

That night in the presbytery sitting-room the canon sat with his two curates and housekeeper. Between sips of port he recounted the events of the day but made no reference to the convent basket or the delighted crows. He waxed eloquently about the simple but incomparable fare given with such a heart and a will by the Flanagans.

'There is nothing on the face of creation,' the housekeeper said solemnly, 'as good as a free-range egg, freshly laid.' Her listeners lifted their glasses in agreement while she rearranged the knitting which lay upon her lap. 'What crowns it all, of course, is fresh brown bread made with expert hands and Sarah Flanagan has years of breadmaking behind her.'

Again the listeners lifted their glasses, this time without drinking from them.

'But,' the housekeeper was continuing as she resumed her knitting, 'if there was homemade butter going with the brown bread you would have a feast fit for a parish priest.'

Here they all laughed, none more so than the canon. The housekeeper smiled to herself when the laughter had abated. She had made the call from her sister's phone and she had adopted a sharp Ulster accent in an effort to conceal her identity. There was no doubt in her mind that she had escaped detection. She had no qualms of conscience about the call. Her primary role in life was to protect her canon against all comers whether bishops, mutinous curates, rampaging reverend mothers or whosoever threatened the canon's well-being. Other executives in the lay world had wives and secretaries to look out for them whereas Canon Coodle, on the threshold of infirmity, was easy prey for assorted parochial predators. She had watched him suffer over the years at the indelicate hands of Mother Francesca, a pampered virago who couldn't fry a sausage properly and who had burned more rashers in her time than any ten women in the parish put together. Of late the housekeeper had noticed a slight decline in the canon's health, especially during the days leading up to Christmas when she knew that the awful prospect of Francesca's cooking was about as much as he could bear. She had made up her mind irreversibly before she left for her sister's on Christmas Day. Nobody else seemed to notice the extreme distress of Canon Coodle. She resolved that something drastic should be done and that she was the one to do it. She knew Joe and Sarah Flanagan as well as she could know anybody. She knew of their genuine regard for Canon Coodle and she knew that the Flanagans would see to his welfare foodwise. She was proud of what she had done. She had won a reprieve for her lord and master and now that the precedent had been established she would ensure that he would never again have to endure the murderous concoctions of Francesca and thus guarantee a longer and less stressful life for her ageing parish priest.

Christmas Eruptions

There are more rows at Christmas than any other time of year but they are rows of shorter duration even if they are rows of greater intensity. Then, of course, I am a man who supports the theory that there can be no true happiness in any household without a flaming eruption now and again.

I am not talking about the joy that comes with the making-up, which is fine in itself. Rather am I talking about the dispelling of those noxious gases which gather over long periods of calm and lassitude. I refer too, of course, to subjugated feelings and dispositions which have turned evil over the course of time as well as all the other ups and downs which assail the human make-up. If these are not unleashed and if they are retained unnecessarily the human spirit will corrode and instead of relationships which are vibrant and vital there will be inevitable stagnation and you will never have the air-clearing, heart-warming confrontations necessary to the successful maintenance of the human system.

People tend to behave too properly at Christmas and where this happens an outbreak of one kind or another is inevitable. Too-proper behaviour is not natural in that it suppresses the mischief and blackguardism inherent in all of us, barring a sainted few.

If this natural mischief is not vented at regular intervals there can only be two consequences, i.e., stagnation or violence, and bad as the latter is the former is even worse because a stagnant home is no home and a stagnant marriage is God's greatest curse. The occasional verbal outbreak, therefore, is a vital ingredient in the successful marriage.

The most dangerous of the Christmas denizens is the common-or-garden senior male of the household. Nearly always he is likely to be a chap who is set in his ways and who may like to lie down quietly after the excesses of Christmas Day. The best treatment for this type of Yuletide invalid is to guide him to a secluded room and to place a Do Not Disturb sign on the door.

If he is suddenly awakened by some accidental intrusion it should be considered a wise manoeuvre to vacate the vicinity of the room where he rests.

Other dangerous denizens are senior married females who have been pushed too far all day and taken for granted over too long a time. The bother here is that outbreaks are totally unpredictable because females tend to suffer silently and give little indication of the explosive scenes which can and do occur as a matter of course in every respectable household.

When these suppressed housewives erupt it is always wise for outsiders to make for the nearest exit until the cataclysm subsides.

Thankfully Yuletide outbreaks, whether male or female, tend to be of short duration. They should be encouraged up to a certain point, however, for the good of the persons in question and for the good of the family as a whole. One of the most devastating Christmas rows ever to occur in the street where I was born happened a short while before the Christmas dinner. We shall call them Tom and Mary.

Tom was sitting by the fire sipping from a glass of whiskey. Mary was sipping from a glass of sherry as was the wont with females at that time.

'Will you have peas or beans with your turkey?' Mary asked politely.

'It's immaterial to me,' Tom responded with equal civility.

'Make up your mind now like a good man for I haven't all day,' said Mary who had been on the go since daybreak attending to the myriad chores which needed her attention.

'I really don't care one way or the other,' Tom persisted.

'Dammit!' said Mary peevishly, 'will you make up your bloody mind,' whereat Tom told her what she could do with the peas and beans, whereat Mary informed him that he was a thankless wretch, whereat Tom smashed his glass against the floor, whereat they harangued each other without mercy and without let-up for a quarter of an hour, whereat they both grew exhausted and fell into each other's arms, whereat all was peaceful again and instead of having peas or beans they had both peas and beans together and a happy Christmas to boot.

www.ingramcontent.com/pod-product-compliance
Lightning Source LLC
Chambersburg PA
CBHW071223260626
47162CB00004B/1405